Paint the Roses Red

LOOKING GLASS SAGA

BOOK FIVE

Paint the Roses Red

TANYA LISLE

SCRAP PAPER ENTERTAINMENT

ISBN-13: 978-1-988911-71-7

Scrap Paper Entertainment
www.scrappaperentertainment.com

Contents

CHAPTER 1

Just a Peek

THERE WAS A time that she dreaded Wonderland coming back into her life, but now Alice found herself anxious to return to it. She had been unable to spend as much time on the other side of the mirror this summer as she wanted and every time she was over here, it felt like more of a vacation than a chore. It was likely due to the amount of time she spent just wandering through the lands, but that wandering was entirely necessary.

Finding Adam had been a first step, but Matt was still out there somewhere, and she didn't have that much longer. There were only so many days left before the Bandersnatch would take her away and she had long ago given up on winning this bet. All she could do now was try to make amends where she could, returning hearts and hopefully returning Adrianna's brother before she vanished and trapped him in Wonderland.

And figuring out how to make Adam come back, but she felt like Tiger Lily would help her on that.

With every heart she returned, Alice felt like Wonderland was getting quieter. It was the opposite of what she expected, so she really should have known it would happen. Those with the sense to avoid the Queen of Hearts and her growing army of people hunting them down did so, and those who did not were taken. Again.

She wandered through the mirror into the White Rabbit's house, a safe place she had grown comfortable entering Wonderland from, but every time she did, it felt like the silence had eyes watching her from the dimly lit room. As comfortable as she had become doing this, it still felt very strange to do so often. The White Rabbit, for one thing, was never here despite it being his house. For another, there was no mob outside the house demanding her head.

It was not so quiet when she came through today. Something was on the roof, the gentle *tap tap tap* echoing down to her as she exited the house. It wasn't a bird, not that any bird in Wonderland would do something like that at anything other than a door. Very rude to tap on a surface that didn't open. But it didn't sound like the tapping was something malicious or particularly dangerous, at least. Or so she thought.

She left the house, waiting for something to try and grab her and ready to run. If nothing else, she could try twisting out in the ways Peter had taught her, but nothing came after her as she walked away, the tapping getting stronger and faster, irritation behind the sound building. She sidestepped her way out of her path and up to the roof, smiling at what she found.

Adam turned to face her, arms crossed and glowering as his foot continued to tap on the roof. He looked much more like he belonged here now, his clothing much more colourful than before, and in many more pieces than he was in at school. For one thing, there was a vest beneath the coat, and she could see a pair of gloves hanging off a belt at his waist.

"Alice," Adam said, shaking his head. "I don't know whether to be grateful you're here or pissed off that you don't stick around these days."

Her smile was plastic, her eyes held open innocently as she prepared to have this conversation again. "I told you," she said. "I've got a family at home. One that's *actually at home.* They're keeping a closer eye on me than they usually do, so I can't really be in here for long anymore. Has anything changed?"

Adam shook his head. "I've been trying to get the hearts, but it's getting impossible," he said. "The Queen of Hearts is going mental. She decided that there are hearts she didn't have on the other side of the tear in the world and she wants all of them, so she's bringing all of Wonderland that she can get her hands on together. She takes hearts faster than I can think to get them out."

"That's a pain," Alice said. "But that's also nothing new. She was going for the river next, right? Didn't you get a chance to get everyone out of there before the Queen showed up?"

"No one here will actually listen to me. It's... I can't do anything about that, I know. Tweedle Dum and Tweedle Dee are useless. They won't work apart, but they do nothing but argue when they're together. The Jabberwocky doesn't scare anyone in Wonderland and he won't leave the Hatter's side. And you know what it's like making the Hatter do anything. It's rude to make people try to leave their homes. People should be left alone in their own home and without the threat of being forced out by these people with no rank. If the Queen were the one doing it, that would be fine—"

"So get the King's order," Alice said.

"I need you to talk to these people, Alice," he said. "I have no idea how to work around what they're talking about. Everyone here is just such a... I don't know how you do it. They're all crazy."

"You could come back," Alice suggested. She stepped off the roof, appearing down on the ground, and Adam jumped down after her. "They aren't on the other side. And Lance has been asking when I was going to drag you back."

"When I pay them back," Adam said. "I owe too many people here too much."

"You don't even like them."

"I still owe them for this much."

"And you don't want to leave Tiger Lily yet?" Alice asked, looking at him and raising an eyebrow. "She won't come back with you, you know. You don't even have to be here. This whole thing is messed up, but she can take care of herself."

"It's got nothing to do with her."

"You need to come back, Adam," she said. "I don't have much longer. When I'm gone, you're never going to be able to get back home again. You'll be stuck here. You and Matt, wherever he is. Have you heard anything? Has Tiger Lily?"

"If she has, she hasn't mentioned it," Adam said. "I don't even know where I'm supposed to look for him. He's nowhere that I've been."

"Maybe he's not in Wonderland," Alice suggested, not for the first time. She frowned, but it was coming closer to the point where she was going to have to accept that Matt was not here. "Even if he did fall into Wonderland with you and Lance, he might have managed to get through the barrier like Tiger Lily and her people, but the other way. He might be in Neverland."

"Tiger Lily hasn't seen him."

"Maybe *you* should be going with her when she goes back. If she ever goes back. She disappears on you and you assume she's there, but she never says she is."

"He can't be in there. It's too dangerous."

"That's the stupidest reason for him not being in there I've ever heard," Alice said. "Do you know how dangerous it is to climb to the roof and get across two buildings on a rope? Which, might I remind you, both of you *did*."

"Actually, that was Lance."

"Are you telling me that Matt *isn't* willing to go across two buildings on a rope?"

"Oh no," Adam said. "That was him. Him and Lance. I had nothing to do with it."

"You did stupid stuff all the time back home," she snapped at him. "Why wouldn't he be doing all the same stuff here? Getting himself into trouble and being impossible to find because he thinks all of this is fun. He could be *anywhere* around here, including being held somewhere by the Queen of Hearts. You were in some castle in the sky I didn't even know about for a long time."

"I liked you better at school," Adam said, looking sidelong at her. "You were a lot more quiet there."

"Are you making people uncomfortable again?" The sly voice said out of nowhere, the Cheshire Cat appearing soon after it. Alice was sure his fur was thinning as time wore on, but his violet eyes continued to shine as he watched her. "Or is he realizing the mask you wear while you are in the land of madness that pretends it is not madness falls away when you enter the place where we wear our madness proudly?"

"Does the King have a plan to disperse the Queen's armies?" Alice asked, eyes staying on Adam. She ignored Cat, despite how he tried to get in her way, lingering in the air by her head. She ducked under him so that she could continue to walk on without having to talk to him any longer. Cat continued to appear at her shoulder, but she refused to so much as look away from straight ahead to avoid him. "He will have some sort of plan to do that. It might be time to actually do it."

"The Mad Hatter has a plan," Adam said. "And the King trusts the Hatter for some reason I will never understand. I can't quite get the full idea out of him, though. He keeps going over it in pieces over tea, and you know how that tends to go. As near as I can tell, he wants to break out all the hearts at once, but that's going to need *you* there so you can put them back before the Queen has a chance to make a move to get them back."

"Of course it does," Alice said. She looked at him, wondering how difficult it would be to drop a mirror on his head to make him head home, but that was a trick she had already failed to pull off. She needed to find another way to force him to go back, but no more ideas would come to her. "Let me know when it's all in place, then. Did you want me to bring any word back home for you?"

"Tell them I'm not dead yet," he told Alice. "And that

I'll figure out getting back soon. I just need to figure this last thing out."

"Last thing being the biggest thing. Lance and Evan said they're going to come in here and drag you back themselves soon."

"Let's see them try," Adam said. He popped something in his mouth and vanished from sight. Alice let him go, disappearing herself a moment later. Someone had to find the last Case brother, and it was her fault they were in here in the first place. The responsibility of getting him back fell on her. Just a couple more places to check before she could rule out Wonderland.

CHAPTER 2

Summer Reading

MS. MILLER WAS a permanent fixture in the house during the days that summer. She was there early every morning with something for Alice to study or look over and took her out of the house more often than Alice could remember. They found themselves out for dinner most nights, Ms. Miller taking her out to a new restaurant many nights or grabbing a quick bite for both of them before catching a movie at one of the cheap theatres in town. Alice didn't even know they had so many theatres such a short drive from her house.

She got a full dose of pop culture from Ms. Miller, the woman catching her up on just about everything she possibly could. One day, she sat Alice down and they watched every Disney movie with their magic and princesses, along with an introduction to superheroes and other bits of science fiction and fantasy that her parents deemed too risky for her delicate mind to absorb. She read books and learned everything she could so she could hopefully recognize the references when they came up at school. And Ms. Miller took it upon herself to show Alice all the places online to go to watch these things herself if she so chose.

Being with Ms. Miller was much better than those days that her parents were home for dinner. Alice rarely saw her parents these days, but she realized quickly why. The few nights that her parents insisted on her being home for dinner, telling Ms. Miller that they needed to create some normalcy at home, were tenser than anything she could remember.

The dinner table stayed perfectly silent. Alice kept her head down, focusing on her food. She did not ask for anything and made no eye contact. Even if she wanted more, as she often did, she refused to look up and did not dare do anything that would draw attention to herself. She was careful to not even allow her knife to squeak across the plate or stab anything too hard with her fork.

Her mother looked like she was close to tears most nights, but it was not from sadness or depression. She knew what that looked like, when she was at her wit's end and she didn't know what to do. No, when she was about to cry at the table she was furious and she glared daggers in her father's direction. She sat much straighter and looked like she was barely keeping a torrent contained. In the hours after dinner when Alice was safely in her room, she would unleash it.

Her father looked generally surly himself, not wanting to engage in any conversation. It felt like as soon as anyone dared to try and speak, a fight would break out. He said nothing, ignoring the looks in his direction, and Alice knew better than to add to them.

Every night of this, Alice ate very slowly and she was careful to be the last person left at the table. Her father looked like he wanted to say something about it, but he was stopped by the glares from her mother and distracted by the upcoming shouting match. Alice was already very good at blocking the sound of them out, and it was easier now that she had access to a computer with headphones.

"Are they going to divorce?" Alice asked Ms. Miller, almost absently. Her eyes did not deviate from her homework. She continued reading through the material and filling out the worksheets, all things that she would not have to actually learn for another year or two at this point, though Ms. Miller saw no reason for her not to get a start on them.

Ms. Miller went very still behind her. "Why do you think they'll do that?" she asked, her words very carefully chosen and deliberately delivered.

"So they are."

"I didn't say that. I don't know what's happening in the relationship, so I can't say what's going to happen with them."

"But they are," Alice said. "What did I do this time?"

"Nothing, Alice. You did nothing."

"I always did something," Alice said. She finished another question, regretting asking already. She wasn't upset that it might finally happen. She had already accepted the possibility back when she was regularly seeing the doctors. She was more curious than anything else, though Ms. Miller was very concerned.

"You are not responsible for your parents' marriage, Alice," Ms. Miller told her. "They are. Whatever happens with them, you are not responsible for anything that happened. They are happy with everything you've done so far. You have been doing well in school and you aren't getting in trouble."

"Our father wasn't happy when I asked to join that club," Alice told her. She was almost done the sheet. "I wonder if they fought over that. I think our mother would have let me go. She wanted Lori to know how to defend herself, so she might have made him mad."

Ms. Miller shook her head and Alice handed her the finished sheet. "Alice, nothing you've done would drive your parents apart."

"They nearly broke up when I was going to all the doctors," she told Ms. Miller. "Mom thought it was silly to keep going to see them when they kept saying there was nothing wrong with me, but Dad insisted we just weren't talking to the right ones yet. They fought a lot back then, too. It's like now. You have to be very quiet when they're both there."

"I'm sure it has nothing to do with you, Alice."

"Maybe."

"If it was, you wouldn't be going back to Lucena in the fall, right?"

Alice stayed quiet, Ms. Miller seeming content at that and going over the worksheet. Alice did well yet again; already so familiar with the material that she doubted she was going to have any problem when they did finally cover it. It probably defeated the purpose of school if she learned everything they were going to teach her now, but that was what Ms. Miller was here for. She couldn't follow her to school and teach her there. And there was an urgency in getting Alice through the material now that Alice didn't want to think about.

"Looks good," Ms. Miller said, smiling down at her and putting the work back on her desk. "What did you want to do today?"

They were out for the whole day, Ms. Miller taking her around downtown Seattle not for the first time to look at the art exhibitions in town and catching a play before dinner. It was late when she finally deposited Alice back home, and her parents were not back yet. Alice took that as a good thing, glad to be spared the yelling for a few more hours at least. Maybe one of them wouldn't be home at all, which would mean she could be spared it entirely for the night.

She got online as soon as Ms. Miller was gone to check her email. She had been keeping in touch with many of the Cases over the holiday so far, most of them unnecessarily worried about her. Evan and Lance were both trying to find out more about Adam and if she had any luck finding Matt yet. She explained as best she could that she hadn't gotten as much of a chance to go with Ms. Miller coming by almost every day. Adrianna just wanted to know what she was doing and Alice found responding to her came easily, telling her about all the places she had seen and things she had done with Ms. Miller, as well as venting about not knowing what to do about her sister.

Lance seemed to know something about Lori, but he never told her anything. It was frustrating how in text he could ignore just about anything that he didn't want to talk about. In return, she started withholding information from both him and Evan, just to make it a little fairer, though it did nothing to persuade him to tell her anything.

Today, she had an email from Adrianna that she hoped would have some good news. It was already the start of August and she had been waiting since the tension in the house made itself felt to find out if Adrianna could have her over. She hadn't asked to be invited, but Adrianna offered at the beginning of the summer when Alice first told her about how tense it was with her parents.

Hi Alice!

My dad finally got hold of your dad! He'll probably tell you, but I'm too excited. He said it's okay for you to come over for the rest of the summer! I think Dad said you'd be here around the end of the week, so only a few more days. We're getting your room ready already.

Adrianna

Alice couldn't help but be excited at the prospect of not being in this house anymore. She might even get more of a chance to go to Wonderland without having both her parents and Ms. Miller to worry about. Keeping track of time in there was getting easier, but hiding how tired the trips left her was a strain. Ms. Miller was suspicious as it was, and Alice sleeping in did nothing to alleviate that.

Still, she wanted to see Adrianna again and she wanted to be in her house. It felt so much warmer and more inviting than her own. She could hardly wait.

The mirror over her dresser loomed in the corner of her eye and she felt a familiar pang of regret. She might have been able to pop over for a bit tonight, but now that she knew her father had agreed, she would have to stay put, just in case he decided to come in to tell her. He might not be home for a while, but to be safe she would have to forego the trip over today, even if it was only for an hour. He couldn't come home to find her room empty. She couldn't pretend she was in the shower for that long and he was being more thorough these days to make sure she was actually under the covers.

Alice sat at her desk and took out a book, waiting. One of her parents would probably be there for her before she went to bed, and she needed to be ready for it. Hopefully it would be the last time she would have to deal with this for a while.

CHAPTER 3

#

TAKING THE PLANE alone was a relaxing experience for Alice. The people around her were nice and left her alone with her book for the trip, only asking if she wanted a drink or snack. She managed to finish off the rest of the *Percy Jackson* series that Ms. Miller had given her for the summer to finish off and she was left wanting more after that last book. She wondered if Adrianna had any recommendations, though she didn't really read for fun like Alice did.

She still didn't know what the big deal was with the fiction that her parents tried so hard to keep her away from. After a full summer of it, she still didn't think there was any more validity to it than before. She knew that none of it was anything that could really happen. Besides, Wonderland was far stranger than anything happening in any of these stories, where things actually made sense, had rules that they all had to follow, and the characters had distinct goals to achieve.

Wonderland gave her none of those things. She was just being thrown around at this point, wondering how long she would be asked to do things until she finally figured out what it was Wonderland wanted from her. It needed to come up with something soon, before she disappeared once and for all. At least she could see an end to everything, and she had tasks to perform until that happened, even if they might not be the correct ones.

When she finally made it off the plane, she found her bags on the conveyer belt and pulled them out, full of supplies for school and a new uniform that was a much better fit for her than the previous one. Alice didn't realize how much she had grown until she saw just how much shorter her old uniform was than her new one. For now, she grabbed the purple suitcase off the conveyor belt and made her way to the exit. She hoped she could find her ride. She wasn't sure which of Adrianna's brothers was coming to pick her up.

It took her a moment before she found Evan casually waiting while a girl next to him with short, bright red hair appeared to be freaking out. She was not happy to be here, that much Alice could tell from her body language, and she kept her face hidden in a way that told Alice that she didn't want to be recognized in this crowd of people. Evan leaned over and said something quietly to her, the other girl seeming to calm down. She turned around to look at Alice, brushing her bangs out of her face and accepting her fate.

Alice got closer and thought there was something very familiar about her in the way she stood. Behind the long red bangs that threatened to fall back over her eyes was a face that wasn't completely dissimilar to her own. She held up a hand and bent her fingers one by one in a sheepish wave that made Alice stop where she stood.

"Lori?" Alice asked no one at all, her voice quiet as she peered at her. It couldn't be. She was supposed to be in England. Not only that, but Lori wasn't allowed to dye her hair or cut it that short. Their father didn't like them having short hair and definitely wouldn't condone such a colour on Lori. And Lori was in England.

Evan went to Alice's side and picked up her suitcase for her as he did on her first day, smiling and pretending that nothing unusual was happening. "Hey Alice," he said. He gently nudged her forward and stayed a step behind her as they got closer, urging her closer to Lori. "How was your flight?"

"Lori?" Alice asked a little more loudly, her blue eyes on Lori and not looking away. It didn't matter that Evan was there at all. "They said you were in England."

"Not quite how it worked out," Lori said. She was being

very careful to avoid meeting Alice's eyes. "How was your flight? And how's school been?"

"It was fine," Alice said. She couldn't believe that Lori was here. Hundreds of questions circled her mind, all of them wanting desperately to burst out, but the look on Lori's face stopped her. She looked nervous, very much like she did when she was in trouble with their father. When that happened, she would run away in tears as soon as they finished talking. Alice didn't want to do that to her, so she let herself ask the least important question. "So does that mean you didn't bring anything back for me?"

The laugh that came out of Lori at that was enough to make Alice relax. It had been a long standing joke that whenever Lori got back from a trip, whether it be something with school or spending a week with friends, she would bring Alice back something as a trinket or treat from the outside, smuggling it in under the utmost secrecy to the point Alice had come to expect it.

"You broke out on your own this time," Lori said with a pat on Alice's head. "God, you got tall while I was gone."

"Two years," Evan offered, his voice staying light and casual. "I imagine you two are going to have a lot of catching up to do. Good thing Addie's out of the house for the rest of the day with Claudia. For some reason she thinks you're not getting in until tomorrow."

"You totally set me up," Lori said.

"It's been going on for long enough, Rayne," he told her. "You can't expect Lance to keep the secret now that he knows. Be grateful that you got that long with him keeping quiet. And that everyone was so accommodating when the blackmail started."

"So Lance knew too?" Alice asked. "Did *everyone* know where you were?" She stopped herself from asking any more than that, already worried that it was too much. If they all knew and didn't tell her... If Adrianna had known...

Lori shook her head, snaking a gentle arm around Alice's shoulders as they walked. "It was supposed to just be Travis and Joe who knew, along with their dad," she said. "And then Evan butted in and figured it out."

"You cut and dyed your hair," Evan told her. "You can't really expect me to ignore that. Not everyone is blind in that house."

"I'd never even met half of you guys," Lori said, her protest weak. "I thought I could get away with it for a little longer than a week."

Evan shook his head and put Alice's suitcase into the car. Alice and Lori piled into the back, a rather large box taking up the front seat. Lori eyed it for a while as she did up her seatbelt and they started moving.

"I should have known you were setting me up."

"It's been long enough," Evan repeated. "Maybe you should be telling Alice where the hell you were instead of accusing me of setting you up, since we've been so good about keeping you up to date about the wellbeing of the little sister you left behind."

"You told her about me?" Alice asked, shrinking back in her seat away from both of them.

From the rear view mirror, she could see Evan smile back at her before they started moving. "Only the important stuff," he said. "Nothing unnecessary, I promise."

Silence lingered in the car and Alice could tell when Evan intentionally slowed down. He kept looking into the backseat, his eyes going to Lori and Lori glaring back at him until she finally turned back to Alice. She let out a deep breath.

"I... Look, our father kicked me out," she told Alice. "Two years ago, he kicked me out of the house and said I wasn't allowed to come back. That's why I haven't been around."

Alice tried to process this. She could see it happening, certainly, but Lori would have had to have done something that really made him mad. "Why?" she asked.

Lori frowned at the question. Alice thought that she might have rehearsed this, but now that it was time to tell her, she couldn't quite get the words out. Her lips parted and closed again, and she looked imploringly at Alice for some way to help her say what she wanted to. She started, her voice emerging, but words were not formed and she was starting to look panicked.

"She wanted to invite her girlfriend over for dinner," Evan suggested helpfully.

"I was getting to that!" Lori snapped at him, looking angrier than Alice had ever seen her. She had tears in her eyes that she was fighting back. "I asked Dad if I could have my girlfriend over for dinner one day and he didn't like that."

"He doesn't like it when we invite people over ever," Alice said, confused. "Does he just really not like her?"

Lori blinked at her and took a very long moment to try to pull herself together. "It's because I'm gay, Alice."

"Oh," Alice said. She thought it over. "So does he just really not like her?"

Evan suppressed a laugh in the front seat as Lori continued to look back at Alice, more confused than she had ever seen her. "He kicked me out because I like girls."

"He didn't know?" Alice asked.

"*You* did?"

"Wasn't I supposed to?"

"How?"

"You're always talking about pretty girls in your class," Alice said. "You're always just friends with the guys. Isn't that how it usually works when you're a lesbian?"

Lori looked at Alice as if she was a puddle of water she had found after wandering a week in the desert without a drink. She reached over the seatbelts and caught her in a tight hug. Alice returned it, though she really wasn't sure what Lori was so happy about.

"I told you that you had nothing to worry about," Evan told her from the front seat.

"So why did he kick you out?" Alice asked after they finally separated.

"Because he doesn't think liking girls is normal," she said, meeting Alice's eyes and looking meaningfully back into them.

Alice nodded. Yes, that would make sense. Their father really didn't like anything that was unusual about them and would rather they be perfectly normal girls, no matter what it took. Alice felt bad for her and understood just about everything about why she'd gone missing now. She had often mentioned to Alice that running away might be a good option to get away from him, so it wasn't that strange that she would do it. It all made pretty much perfect sense, except for exactly where she'd been, which Alice was sure she was about to find out.

"At least he didn't send you to the doctors to fix you," Alice said.

"He did give me that choice," Lori said with a bit of a laugh, though it was hollow and tinged with that sadness that

Alice knew too well. "I figured you'd tell me it was a bad idea, though." She shook her head and let out a sigh before she continued. "Travis convinced his dad to let me stay as a housekeeper. He said I still had to go to school and I could help out Claudia when she needed it in exchange for room and board. I had to get another job to pay for anything that wasn't essential."

"So you've just been living over here?" she asked. "But I was here last year. I came by for Christmas."

"Alice, you know why I couldn't tell you."

Alice knew that look. She thought she was doing the right thing to help her and she shouldn't question it. She had done it to protect Alice. If their father found out that Alice had been in touch with Lori, there was a chance she would be seen as disobedient, especially since Alice wasn't even supposed to mention her. She would be in trouble for just talking to her, likely pulled out of school over it and, if she ever mentioned it again, she might head back to the doctors.

"Yeah," Alice said, looking down in acceptance.

"That's it?" Evan asked from the front seat. "You can't get even a little mad at her? She's put me through a lot of trouble to keep this secret."

"And it should have stayed a secret for a little longer," Lori said, shooting a glare at the back of his seat. "Now there's one more thing to not talk about."

"I swear, Rayne, between this and the cameras and everything else I've heard about your parents, I keep thinking you live in a horror movie. All you need now is a dead sibling and you're set."

"Arthur," both Lori and Alice said at the same time. Lori continued, "He died before I was born. Mom and Dad don't really like to talk about it."

"I'm going to shut up now," Evan said.

Alice couldn't help but smile at that, Lori joining her. "You might have noticed that he's calling me Rayne," she said. "I've been going by Rayne for a while now. You can still call me Lori, though."

"I missed you," Alice said. "I didn't know what happened."

"I tried to get them to keep an eye on you for me. Evan pulled a few strings and got you a room with his sister. She talks about you sometimes. It seems like the two of you are getting along pretty well and you're adjusting just fine without me."

"But what have you been doing?" Alice asked. "You're living in their house and going to another school and having a whole life while you've been gone."

"I'm actually living in a little apartment on their estate right now," Lori told her. "I think it's, like, a converted servant's quarters or something. It's nice, though. And I'm off at public school. It's not as bad as Father Dearest thought it was. A bit weird and tough to get used to, but it's not that bad. The people are nice enough and I'll graduate on time, I think. And I'm kind of seeing someone."

"Someone different?" Alice asked. "Do I get to meet her?"

"Maybe later," Lori said. "I haven't exactly…"

"It's okay," Alice said. There was already so much else what had happened that Alice could wait to meet other people that Lori now had in her life. She hadn't even known any of Lori's friends before now. "Maybe next time."

"How are our parents?" she asked. The question seemed to pain her, but she powered through it anyway. "I heard that they weren't doing so hot lately."

Alice looked at her sideways. "How?"

"After I heard you got in trouble last year, I got in touch with Ms. Miller," she said. "It sounds like it wasn't too bad this time around, but I just wanted to be sure."

"Not bad?" Evan demanded, speaking from the front seat again. "How is being locked in your room all day with no access to food or anything else considered not bad?"

"I thought you said you were shutting up."

"I don't know," Alice said. "It's like… remember back when our father couldn't find a doctor that would say there was something wrong with me? And our mother just wouldn't talk to him and every time someone said something, they just started screaming?"

"Yeah, back when everything was about you. I got off pretty easy back then."

"I think they might actually divorce this time, though," Alice said. "At least last time, they could just find a doctor and that was the end of it. I don't know what the problem is this time. When they start yelling, they aren't yelling at me anymore, so I don't know. You think it's me?"

"Nope," Lori said, sounding almost cheerful about it. "This time it's me."

"I'm going to stop both of you before you make me call child services," Evan said, pulling into the driveway and stopping at the small house on the side of the Case's larger house. "You two keep doing your thing and being horrifying in Rayne's place. I'll take your stuff up to the guest room."

"Thanks, Evan," Lori said, getting out of the car. Alice followed after her a moment later, heading into the small house. It was a one-level building with a loft where Lori kept her bed, currently strewn with clothing. Below was the living room, kept messy as Alice remembered with posters on the wall that had very familiar faces on them from Lori's room. There were wires littered around the place with half-made jewelry and a list printed out with designs sitting on the coffee table.

"Sorry it's a mess," Lori said, clearing a spot off the couch for Alice to sit. "I'll make some tea."

Alice took a seat, plopping down and watching as Lori went around to her small kitchen to get tea together. She was still nervous, Alice could tell, but Alice didn't know why. Alice wasn't mad at her, though she supposed she probably should be. Lori did leave her to the mercy of their parents without her protection right as she was starting at school, then to start Lucena Academy on her own, but it had turned out fine.

"So you've been keeping an eye on me this whole time?" Alice asked. "You didn't have to. I'm okay. Really."

"I had to," Lori said. "I'm sorry I left you behind with them. I should have tried to get you out of there, but I wasn't able to do anything about it. And I wanted to email you or something, but I don't know if our father installed anything on the computer or if he got your password somehow and he might be checking that. And I just... I couldn't go back, Alice. I'm sorry. I couldn't go back."

"It's okay," Alice told her again. "I can handle myself. I know what I'm doing now." She accepted the tea from Lori and Lori sat down next to her. "And he did have a bunch of stuff put on my computer, but I got Lance to take a look at it and he took everything off."

"Well, that's good," Lori said. "Lance is a good kid. They all are."

"I still can't believe they kicked you out," Alice said. Lori picked up some pliers and started to bend the metal wires of one of her designs, working on the next of the necklaces that she had printed out on a piece of paper on the table. "They actually liked you."

"They liked me less than you think," Lori told her. "Those cameras in the hall weren't so much for *you* as they were to make sure I stopped breaking out of the house at night. And during the day. And every other time. Father doesn't like me going out unsupervised."

"He doesn't like a lot of things," Alice agreed.

There was a knock at the door and Lori got up to open it. Travis was on the other side, looking frantic. "Rayne, they're setting you up," he said quickly.

"I know," she said, pointing inside the room and at Alice. Alice smiled and waved back at him, Travis looking flustered. "No more dealing with Lance's blackmail, I guess."

"Hi Alice."

"Hi," Alice said back, smiling.

"Did you want to come in?" Lori asked, moving aside. "I just made some tea."

"Sure?" Travis said. He entered, taking an awkward seat on the floor across from Alice. "Wasn't expecting you until tomorrow. How was the flight?"

Alice continued to smile at him. "It was good. I finished my book. I don't know what I'm going to pick up next, though."

"What book?" Lori asked.

"*The Last Olympian*. It's the last one in the *Percy Jackson* series."

"*Our* parents let you read that?" Lori asked, looking genuinely impressed.

Alice shook her head, smiling and reaching into her bag. There was a Pride and Prejudice cover over the copy she had. "Of course not. Ms. Miller's been sneaking them to me with different covers on them. They don't even know what I'm doing these days."

"Good girl," Lori said, giving Alice a pat and going back to her wire work. "With any luck, after the parents finally split, Mom turns out to be decent away from Dad and you'll get to actually put those on your shelf with the right covers on them."

"So you know for sure your parents are breaking up?"

"Probably," Alice said. "They keep arguing when they talk and it's really tense in the house right now, so I think they will this time. But I don't know about putting them on my shelf, Lori. You think she would?"

"Mom never liked this fiction ban Dad put on you," she said. "She didn't even like the doctors. But you know how Dad is."

"Evan might be onto something with that child services thing."

"My father has lawyers that will somehow turn you into a sex offender if you try to do anything," Lori said. "It happened to at least one of Alice's doctors when he tried to convince our father that there was nothing wrong with her. If I remember right, that's when he found the one that agreed with him."

Alice shrugged, not remembering. She wouldn't have been surprised. Her father really did like suing people for things when they disagreed with him.

"And now I'm uncomfortable," Travis said, looking away. "You're not mad at us for not telling you we knew where she was this whole time, are you?" he asked, looking back at Alice.

Alice shook her head. "It was for the best," she said. "My father wouldn't have liked it if Lori got in touch with me if he found out. But I know not to tell him now that I do know, so it's all right."

"And that's the only thing?" he asked, seeming to want her to say something else. She was at a loss as to what. She let him continue to give her that prying look like he was waiting for a secret password.

"Everything's good," Lori chimed in. "She already knew. She's much more observant than I give her credit for."

"Already knew what?" Alice asked.

"Nothing, Alice," Lori told her, though there was obviously something she was missing. "I've already heard a lot from these guys, but why don't you tell me about what's been happening since I went missing? I get the feeling that they didn't quite give me the full story."

Alice smiled, happy to have her back and preparing a version of the story mentally that would omit anything that had to do with the Jabberwocky, Wonderland, or the Bandersnatch. At this point, the Bandersnatch could take her away forever and she would be fine with it. She found Lori again after she had accepted that it was never going to happen.

"Well," Alice started carefully, careful not to let anything slip. "I met a lot of really nice people at school."

CHAPTER 4

Investigating

THE CASE HOUSE was as big and hectic as she remembered it. Ryan wasn't here, but he was the only one missing. Once Lori brought her back to the house for dinner, they all seemed to want to know about her flight, all surprised to see her here already. The only people who knew she was there at all were limited to Evan, Travis, and Lance.

"I still can't believe you set me up," Lori said, shooting a glare at Evan. "And with *him!* Actually, you I'm not surprised about."

"Sucks that I can't keep getting stuff from it, though," Lance said. "But seriously, that's messed up. You can't just *do* that to someone."

"I think Joe knew something too," Alice said quietly to her, peering over at the smirk on Joe's face as he worked through his plate. He looked like a hooligan again, but he couldn't quite shake that look that he knew more than he was letting on.

"Nope," Joe said. "I had no idea Alice was coming in today. I *may* have seen something about a flight itinerary and saw the two of them conspiring, but I came across no details."

"And you didn't tell me," Travis said. "My own brother."

"So are they," Joe reminded him, laughing. "Besides, Lance was running out of small things to demand. It was about to get ridiculous."

"If you guys had just gone and told her in the first place, you wouldn't have had to do anything!"

"I still can't believe Rayne is your sister!" Adrianna said from next to her. "You've been looking for her for such a long time."

Adrianna was more happy for Alice than annoyed that Alice didn't come to see her first or tell her she was going to be early. Rayne, apparently, had never mentioned anything about a sister to her either, and her identity was coming as a bit of a surprise. Alice was just happy that Lori had a good place to stay during the last couple years.

"I finally know where she is!" Alice said happily. "But what about you?"

The two of them chatted through dinner while Lori accused several people of setting her up, neither sister divulging any embarrassing stories about their childhoods for anyone who asked. Evan stayed very quiet about the whole thing, looking significantly scarred from the car and worried that he already knew far too much. Alice wasn't sure why he looked so traumatized from it all. He wasn't the one who had to go through with it.

Lori had to head out for something after dinner, so Alice retreated to her own room with Adrianna and discussed the new year coming and what they'd heard from everyone. Apparently Adrianna was much better at keeping in touch. Kevin texted her throughout the summer, as did Robert, though he was much more sporadic. His family were doing a lot of events for his father's job as governor, so he was supposed to be on his best behaviour. Heather said little and Sarah kept an Instagram feed going that Adrianna followed and commented on frequently.

"Kevin said he's got someone staying at his house this summer," Adrianna said. "One of his father's friends left their son there, so he's been hanging out with him all summer. I think his name is Peter."

"Do people do that?" Alice asked. "Just leave kids with friend's families when they don't even know their kids? I mean, it's not like he's close or something, right?"

Adrianna shrugged. "Apparently he's coming to Lucena in the fall. It sounds like Kevin just picked up a brother, but

I don't think he likes him very much. He thinks Peter's kind of weird."

"I'd think a random new person who was suddenly my brother was weird too," Alice said. She pulled out the red book and started to go back to transcribing it on her computer while they talked, putting as much of the information on there as possible.

Adrianna looked back at the closed door to Alice's room. "So," she said finally, leaning in close and not looking at the book or the computer screen Alice was working on, "have you been going back there?"

Alice shook her head. "I haven't been able to," she said, feeling upset about it all over again. "I can only go for an hour sometimes. My parents keep coming home early and they come in and check on me. And Ms. Miller was there the whole time I was, so she was there taking me out to do stuff and I couldn't get away with her around either. It's been so hard, and every time I go, Adam always has bad news about what's going on. He won't come back either, no matter how much I talk to him."

"He'll come around," Adrianna said. "He probably just wants to save something before he comes back. He does that sometimes."

"It's getting dangerous," Alice said. "They're starting to round people up and the Queen of Hearts is raising an army.

I think she wants to try to get into Neverland. And I don't know what I'm supposed to do about that. Do I have to stop them? Do I have to let them go so that then all the bad stuff is out of Wonderland? I don't get what I'm supposed to do with any of this."

"I think you're supposed to get rid of the Bandersnatch first, right?" Adrianna said. "That way you'll have time to figure everything else out. And then you can try to get Adam to come back over. He'll come back eventually, so maybe you just have to give him some time. Or you can bring me over and I can try to make him come back for you."

"I am not bringing you over," Alice told her. "It's way too dangerous. You'll get your heart ripped out if you aren't careful."

"I'll be careful," Adrianna said. "I can just eat a tart like you did and then I'll be able to do the disappearing thing too and it'll be fine, right? It'll be fine. And then I can get Adam out myself and you won't have to worry about him anymore."

Alice shook her head, smiling. Adrianna did want to help, she knew, but it was such a bad idea and she didn't understand why. Alice wasn't sure what to say and kept her eyes on the document in front of her, working through the words and references as best she could. "Maybe I'll slip over tonight for a bit," she said. "I might be able to find something good over there."

"I don't think they'll like that."

"Who?"

Adrianna looked back at the door again. "Evan and Lance don't want you going back there while you're here," Adrianna told her. "They think it's too dangerous and Evan's worried your dad will get mad at us if you get stuck over there while you're staying at our place. I mean, you do kind of stay over there for a while sometimes. And Rayne's going to notice now if you're gone for a long time."

"Maybe," Alice said. "I guess I'll keep out for now. Still have all this stuff from Tiger Lily's book to work through. There's so much stuff in here and I can't quite figure out what I'm going to need later."

"What's in it?"

Alice and Adrianna spent the evening talking about the book until they both were too tired to keep going. Alice had been through the book before, but she had been so drugged that she could barely comprehend what was in it. Now, however, she was finding things in there that she could use. There were ways to put people back together after they had been broken apart and make it so they would never break again. If Humpty Dumpty kept complaining about how fragile he was, she could do something about that with just a few extra parts.

Alice waited until the sun broke over the horizon in the morning to go back to Wonderland, now a week after the last time she slipped through the mirror. She was far more inclined to do so early, before anyone had woken up to come and find her. She changed quickly and she climbed through the mirror into the White Rabbit's house.

It didn't feel as quiet today when she got through the mirror. There was something else there with her and she was ready to run back through the mirror already. She didn't want to have to get stuck here for too long and deal with everyone else not knowing where she was back at Adrianna's house. Evan would likely get very mad knowing that she went through and risked her father's wrath on them. Still, she needed to come back and check on Wonderland, at least for a little bit.

She found the disturbance curled up in the corner. Someone was sleeping there, which struck her as completely strange. People in Wonderland didn't sleep. It was never even night here, and none of the people needed it. Even Adam seemed to be perfectly fine without it, but from the way they didn't move, Alice could only assume this person was sleeping.

Unless he was dead. But Alice had also never seen anyone dead in Wonderland either.

She approached cautiously, not sure what to make of it. He was curled up on the floor in the corner, not moving and facing away from her. He looked entirely too familiar from the back and he was lying perfectly still. He was so small, too, and dressed in tatters.

"Oh, you are back," Tiger Lily said behind her. She had someone else on her back, this time one of her people, and laid him down on the ground next to the child. "We will need your assistance. We have encountered a problem."

"What's going on?" Alice asked.

"These," Tiger Lily said, indicating the bodies. "The Queen of Hearts has been trying to build her army and it is not working as well as she believed it would."

Alice crept over to look at the man Tiger Lily just put down. His eyes opened and he curled around himself in the fetal position. Cradled in his hands, he held his heart, bloody and still beating. The hole in his back did not bleed or look like much of anything at all, just dark and vacant instead of filled with organs and flesh as Alice would have assumed. It was like how Wonderland's people were, except his eyes were completely vacant, staring down at his heart like he couldn't believe it was out of his body.

"They live," Tiger Lily told her. "But they do not really live."

Alice touched him, finding him still warm and breathing. She had wondered what would happen if someone outside of Wonderland had their heart stolen, but she hoped that it would work out the same way as when those of Wonderland lost them. They would become dull and obedient instead of whatever this was. With his eyes open, it was hard to think of him as sleeping.

She looked back over at the first body. There was a boy there, the small pirate boy that was trapped in the Queen's dungeon from before. He also gripped his heart, his hole in the front of his chest. He looked pale, the look of terror stuck on his face like he thought he was dying. He very well might be.

"Alice," Adam's voice said. He also had a body with him and Alice was left not knowing what to do with seeing more. "Good timing. You know how to put hearts back, right?"

"I know how to put them back into Wonderland people," she said, looking at the person on his back. It was another one of Tiger Lily's people and she looked back at Tiger Lily. She kept herself composed, not sure what else she was supposed to do at this point but continue to be strong. "I can try to do it for them too. What's going on?"

"The Queen of Hearts," Adam said. "She's been trying the same thing with Neverland refugees as Wonderland folks. It's not taking so well."

"I mean, where are you finding these people?"

"They've been dumping the people who don't fit out in the forest," Adam said. "Tiger Lily thought we should start bringing them here so that you could take a look at them the next time you came. We've only just started to find them."

"Do something," Tiger Lily told her. "There are many more. And the White Rabbit will not appreciate that his house will become a grave if you can do nothing."

"I'll try," Alice said. She looked down at the small child first, not sure where to even begin with him. There was the heart, but she couldn't get it out of his hands. She reached down for it, but as soon as she drew too close, he curled up around it more tightly, protecting it from her.

That was fine. She didn't need to do that. There was something she could do. The words came out of her like an apology easy to fall off of her lips, and her hands followed the familiar patterns to bring the heart back into place. It should have been easy, but it wasn't working this time.

The heart would not leave the boy's hands, no matter how she tried to force it out of them. The connection would not be made and she could not feel the bond forming the same way that it did in those from Wonderland. She didn't know what kept it from going, but she felt like she was doing something very wrong. She missed something important in how Neverland worked, and that kept it from working.

She kept trying, straining herself to keep making it go, but she could not convince the boy to release his heart, or even to put it back in himself. He did not trust her to do what needed to be done, she could sense, and he wanted to put it back himself, though he didn't know how. She didn't know how to make it work for him, though, and she was getting very tired trying to make it work.

Adam pulled her back when she started to feel shaky on her feet. "Alice!" he snapped at her. "Stop!"

From the look on his face and how tired she felt, Alice wondered how long she had been trying it. She felt drained and like she needed to go back to sleep for another night in order to recover.

"Let her continue," Tiger Lily told him. "She must figure out how to save my people."

"I don't think she owes you anything," Adam told her, a dark look in his eye as he said so. Tiger Lily did not falter, but she did not continue her protest either as Adam turned back to Alice. "You're at my house now, right?" he asked. "You should probably go back. Someone will probably notice you gone before long."

"Yeah," she said distantly. She was so tired. "Hey, did you know my sister was living at your house all this time?"

"What?"

"Yeah," Alice said, letting him walk her back to the mirror. She felt dizzy, but the words kept coming out. "Rayne. That's Lori. She was apparently staying with you guys after my parents kicked her out of the house."

"Just get back, Alice," Adam said, shoving her back through the mirror. She hit the glass at first, forgetting what she was supposed to be doing with it before she finally made her way back through. That feeling of tugging, of the boy resisting her attempts to put his heart back, lingered with her and she was tired despite still feeling it.

Alice shook her head as she walked through the mirror and back into her room. As soon as her head was back through, though, she knew there was going to be a lot more trouble for her. Not only was the sun lighting up the room brightly, but Lori was backing away from the mirror and trying not to say anything. She shook her head, her eyes wide and desperately refusing to acknowledge what she was seeing as she watched Alice come out.

"Hi," Alice said awkwardly as she crawled the rest of the way out of the mirror. She had to think quickly, to find a way to make Lori not pay any attention to anything she had just seen. To make her think that she had seen nothing at all. "I'm sorry, I didn't hear you. Is it late already?"

"What is that?" Lori asked, her voice very quiet as Wonderland faded away from behind her. She kept her eyes on the mirror even after it wasn't showing anything of the White Rabbit's house and she didn't know how to process it. She wouldn't have seen anything except a room with Tiger Lily, Adam, and three unconscious bodies, but Alice wondered if the mirror showed everything while she was over there.

"It's a mirror," Alice said.

"There was something in there," Lori said. "*You* were in there. You came out of the mirror."

"I wouldn't be in a mirror," Alice said. "That's silly. I'm not allowed to be silly. And it's not possible for someone to come out of a mirror. I was just sitting on the counter for a minute."

Lori shook her head, straightening up. "Nope," she said. "No. This is not happening. Nope." She turned and walked very quickly out of Alice's room.

Alice went after her, still feeling drained but needing to. For one thing, she couldn't have Lori getting mad at her, not now that she'd just found her again. For another, she couldn't have her telling Evan or someone else that she'd been heading into Wonderland under their roof. They would not be happy with her if they found out, and she didn't want Adrianna to know either. She needed to make sure Lori forgot all about it, rather than just denying it for now and telling someone about what she thought she saw later.

"Lori!" she called after her once she got out of her room. Lori had already gone into another room by the time Alice was in the hall, not catching where she'd gone. She looked around the hall, making her way slowly down it and trying to figure out where she might have turned. "Lori?"

She kept going down the hall until she found an open door that intrigued her. It was the only one that was open, and Lori didn't always remember to close the door when she was upset. Maybe...

It felt like a whole other world inside the room. As old as Adrianna's house sometimes felt, she never expected it to ever have a room that felt this old. The interiors were dark with the curtains drawn and there were faint outlines of several things that she didn't think were actually here. She could have sworn that she saw dead animals hanging from the ceiling, but the pungent scent of overgrown plants overwhelmed any scent of decay. What little sunlight came through the window illuminated shapes and gave her the feeling that she'd walked into an old witch's hut, but it felt much more regal than that. There was a familiar feeling in here that a hut would not convey. It felt like power and like something she knew all too well. Something that still haunted her nightmares.

It was like the Queen's room of hearts, less all the hearts.

Perched at the far side of the room, Alice thought she saw something that might be books. She reached for the light switch on the wall, hoping that she could get a better idea of what was in here. If she was fast, she could take a look around and get out before anyone noticed a thing.

The light showed a very different room. It looked like an office and craft room, with dried flowers hanging and pieces of fabric all over the place. It also looked like it was used regularly, the counters cluttered but free of dust. Against the far wall was a piece of work in progress and a book open for reference on it.

Alice blinked at the change, certain her eyes weren't playing tricks on her before but not sure what else she was supposed to see here. She walked through the room quickly, still feeling that sense that there was something in here that shouldn't be here. Most of the fabrics scattered around the room didn't look like they went together or like they were part of an individual project, more that they were there to make it look like there was something being made here.

She found the thing that was out of place at the far side of the room. The book being used for reference wasn't a book for sewing, but a thing that didn't belong in here or in Wonderland at all. It was an old book with a cover that looked like it was made of leaves. She decided that it shouldn't still be as green for how dead those leaves felt under Alice's fingers as she picked the book up. The open page outlined the finer details of what mustika pearls could do.

It couldn't stay here, that much was certain. She couldn't leave it for someone else to find and do something with. It was probably the thing causing this room to play such strange tricks, as no one in this house would be able to do anything with it. Adrianna couldn't even look at the book without getting a headache, and her brothers didn't seem to know anything about magic either.

She couldn't leave it here.

Alice went to the light switch and turned it off, the room reverting back to that look and feel of a very large and regal witch's hut. Another step and she was back in her room, taking the book with her and putting it with the rest.

CHAPTER 5

Unespected Reunion

LORI SAID NOTHING the rest of the break about what she walked in on. Alice accepted that as good enough. Lori still spent plenty of time with both her and Adrianna, the three of them hanging out a lot over the last two weeks of vacation. They had lots of adventures with the Case family when their father was around, as well as when he wasn't.

Alice did not so much as look at the books for the rest of the time there, nor did she dare head back into the mirror. She didn't want Lori accidentally catching her again. She never knocked and Alice worried that the others might stop doing that as well. She was not safe with doing it until she was back at school where there was a door that she felt comfortable locking.

Alice knew this was going to be her last year at school. One way or another, she wasn't going to see next year. Unless the green book and the red book came together and, though the miracle of Christmas colours, gave her an answer, she was going to disappear at the end of this school year. She would certainly try to make it all work out, but she was going to have to focus a lot more on making sure that everything she needed to do was done before the end of the year.

Adam needed to come back. Matt needed to get back. She had found Lori and she was doing well for herself. Sarah had come back and seemed well as well. She should probably try to repair the rip between Wonderland and Neverland before anything else came through and tried to make things horrible for those left behind. If she could get all of that done then it would be fine to fall to the Bandersnatch.

Ten months. She could handle this. There had to be an easier way to find Matt, though. She would probably have to take a bit of time over the break to go back to look through Neverland for him again, or at least enlist Adam to help instead of his crusade to save Wonderland.

She wondered if she could teach Tiger Lily to return hearts. She should leave someone behind who could do that. If she wasn't around to do that, then there should be *someone* else who could take over in her place. She would prefer to leave it to someone from Wonderland, but she doubted any of them would be able to focus long enough to learn how.

Even if she didn't manage to get it all done, she could hope that it would all work out. Wonderland would be able to find someone else who was able to do it. Wonderland didn't really need her. The hero of Wonderland stuff that the Bandersnatch said was nonsense. It could probably just pull someone else in to fix the problems if it really wanted to.

For all she knew, Wonderland actually wanted to be taken over by these books.

She settled in early nonetheless once they were back in the dorms, feeling very much like there was a clock ticking down as she unpacked the rest of her stuff. She might not even have to deal with her things for much longer. Alice contemplated just going crazy and acting out for the year, enjoying herself and generally having fun, but she did need to make it to the end of the eight months. That impulse would have to wait.

For now, she left the books in her suitcase and went with Adrianna next door to visit Sarah and Heather. She smiled at Sarah's side of the room, glad to have her back regardless of the circumstances that brought her there. Since she'd been dumped over the summer, she returned to her old self and Alice felt like things were getting back to normal around here.

She wondered if anything would really change with her gone. Nothing much changed with Sarah gone except for the lack of someone trying to hook them up with someone or try to get them a makeover. Robert looked a little lonely as well, but really there wasn't much difference with her gone. Alice would be fine gone, leaving her friends with no memories of her and therefore no reason to mourn.

"You need a phone, Alice," Sarah said after a while. "I was in Seattle for a week this summer and I had no way to get in touch with you."

"You could have emailed," Alice told her.

"You take so long to get back, though," she said. "Seriously. Just ask your parents for a phone or something. Or actually turn on Skype during the summer."

"I'm not supposed to be on the computer too much."

"So?" Sarah asked, looking like she didn't understand what was going on. She shook her head and let out a sigh. "Whatever, you probably weren't there at the time anyway. Adrianna said you went to stay with her. And there was something about a sister?"

"Yeah," Alice said. "It turns out my sister was working at Adrianna's house this whole time."

"Travis knew," Adrianna said. "And Evan knew. Joe knew. And Lance found out at some point. Oh, and Dad knew! They just never said anything."

"Your families are weird," Heather told them. "But at least neither of you got a new brother over the summer out of nowhere."

"Is that what actually happened?" Sarah asked. "He said something about it, but I thought he was being dramatic or it was some Asian thing or something. Is it actually, like, an actual new family member or what?"

"Kevin's thing?" Alice asked. "He said something about it in an email, but it was weird."

"No, apparently it's a legit thing," Heather told them. "He thought his dad was just watching a friend's kid, but then he went ahead and adopted him instead. He spent the summer in some sort of accelerated learning thing with Kevin showing him how to do stuff so he could come to school this year. It's been a bit crazy for him, I think, and now he's supposed to keep an eye on him or something. He's got no idea what happened and the kid doesn't know how to tell him what's going on either."

"Peter, wasn't it?" Sarah asked. "I think he said his name was Peter. You don't think this means we're going to have to hang out with him, do you?"

"If he is, he'll have to pull his own weight around here," Heather said. "He can start tutoring Rob with that fancy Korean education."

They continued chatting until they got bored and headed out into the foyer, finding Robert and Kevin at the bottom of the stairs, Robert talking more than Kevin. Kevin kept shaking his head and looking like he could barely believe anything he was saying.

"There they are," Kevin interrupted as soon as the girls

got close enough to join them. "We were wondering if you guys were even showing up for the assembly."

"If only we could skip it," Heather said. "So where's this new brother of yours?"

"Peter's trapped by his roommate," Kevin said, pointing a small ways across the foyer. "And no," he said, turning to Heather, "I still don't know how I managed to get a brother in under nine months. Stop asking. I'll introduce you guys." Kevin caught his eye and waved him over.

Peter was light and springy on his feet, looking more comfortable in the group of people and full of smiles. He was a dark child, sprite-like in his features and confident in his stride, though the uniform looked far too formal for him. But when he caught sight of Alice, he had a momentary look of panic and was very careful to avoid meeting her eyes again.

Alice went very still in that instant when their eyes met. Peter. It was Peter. Neverland Peter. She couldn't quite wrap her head around how Neverland Peter managed to get out of Wonderland or what he was doing here. She wasn't sure if he was going to be like Cat, making her life miserable or... No, that was the only thing she could think he might be doing. He was probably here to try and convince her to go save Neverland for him from whatever horrible thing that black book he talked about was doing to it. The zombies he left roaming through the land were not her problem and she wouldn't let them be.

"Guys, this is Peter," Kevin said. "Peter, Sarah, Heather, Alice, and Adrianna."

"Hi," he said, smiling sweetly back at them in a greeting that was a little too rehearsed. Alice could tell, but she made no move to call him out on it just yet. She needed to wait and see what he was going to do before she did anything.

"He's a year younger than us," Kevin continued. "I have no idea what else I need to tell them about you."

"That's fine," Peter said, his eyes suddenly darting up to Alice and then smiling. "I need to talk to you. Right now."

Alice found herself very suddenly being dragged away by Peter, much to the surprise of everyone else standing with them. Alice was too startled to do anything and no one made any attempt to stop Peter as he pulled her away until they were just outside the door and out of the way of the prying ears that might overhear them. Alice pulled away from him before they got too far, stopping both of them and turning back around on him.

"What was that?" she demanded.

"You're pretending you don't know me. You know who I am. You were going to save Neverland for—"

"*Stop!*" Alice hissed at him. Peter was going to make

things very difficult for her, she could already tell. "You can't talk about Wonderland out here like that."

"Wonderland?"

"Neverland." Alice took a deep breath and tried to keep herself calm. She had to keep herself together to get through this. At least Cat wasn't social. Peter was off talking to other people as well, attending as an actual student with a room-mate and classes instead of lounging in a tree all day, which was going to make it difficult for her if he let anything slip about her. "You just can't talk about them with people around like that."

"But there's no one around here," Peter said, his voice not remotely quiet. "And you know about Neverland, so why not? I know I can't talk about it around Kevin, because Wiggles is Mr. Seok now and he won't let me at home when anyone else but him is around, but—"

"*No*," Alice told him, her voice firm and her eyes boring into his to keep him paying attention. "No talking about it. Not ever. As far as anyone is concerned, we never met and we don't know each other. Just pretend everything that happened before didn't happen and we never met."

"I thought girls weren't supposed to lie," he said, looking at her funny.

"Just don't tell anyone anything about Neverland," she

said. "Or anything about me. Please, at least don't tell them about me. Okay?"

Peter let out a loud, exaggerated sigh. "Girls are so weird," he said, floating backwards. His body became horizontal, floating through the air.

Alice reached forward and grabbed him by the foot, yanking him back down onto the ground. "And no flying!"

"You are no fun, Alice," he said, putting his feet properly back on the ground and dusting off his uniform that was devoid of anything that needed dusting off.

Alice stormed off, walking away from that potential bit of trouble and joined everyone else a moment later inside. They weren't there long, Kevin ushering them all to move towards the assembly while apologizing to her.

"Sorry," he said. "Peter's kind of weird. If he starts doing anything strange, just ignore it. Did he say why he wanted to talk to you?"

"He thought I looked like someone," Alice said. It was true, in a sense. He thought that she looked like Alice, the girl in Wonderland who he drafted into saving Neverland for him because he didn't want to deal with the zombies anymore.

Kevin shook his head. "If he starts calling you Wendy, let me know," Kevin said. "Just try to put up with him for a bit. I don't know what his deal is exactly, but he's still adjusting to being around people, I think. He keeps coming up with all these stories and I don't know what I'm supposed to do with him."

"Nothing," Heather told him. "You're new to the older sibling thing. Trust me. If the little ones start going a little crazy, you let them be crazy. And when they start realizing that the crazy doesn't work so well, you laugh at them. And when they stop crying, *then* you help them out."

"You are a terrible older sister," Sarah said, bumping into Heather lightly. "You make me so glad I'm an only child."

"I am a *great* older sister," Heather said. "My brother learned the hard way not to get into my stuff." She pounded a fist into her hand and smiled, happy to demonstrate.

Alice barely paid attention to the assembly, too distracted by the presence of Peter in her life again. She needed to figure out a way to keep him from talking about her. She would be fine with him making everything difficult for himself with his flying and stories about whatever it was he knew about Neverland, but Alice did not want to deal with being brought into these stories herself.

She didn't even know how he got here or what he was doing here in the first place. There might be a way out of Neverland that was different from how she got in and out of Wonderland, but that was even more concerning. The Queen of Hearts might find out that there was a way out that she could use. Anyone in Wonderland might, and if they did, she didn't trust that they wouldn't immediately try to find her in the process.

"So how did you get him exactly?" Sarah asked Kevin quietly next to her, the assembly more or less forgotten between them. "Like, he just showed up one day?"

Kevin shook his head. "Dad brought him home from work one day," he said. "He just said Peter was going to be staying with us for a while. At first I felt really bad for him. He looked like he was terrified and he just wasn't sleeping at all, but he was also doing a lot of weird stuff too." Kevin looked over at the sea of heads towards him for a moment as if debating on whether or not to elaborate. He decided against it. "About a week later, when he looked like he's going to fall over from not sleeping for so long, Dad says that he's going to become a permanent part of the family. I think he was scared that my dad was going to make him go back to wherever he came from, but he started to calm down after he found out he was staying."

Kevin shook his head again and took his eyes off of him, directing them back at the stage. "He's really weird sometimes. I mean, he calls Dad Wiggles sometimes and Dad just goes with it and thinks it's funny, but I don't think he deserves to go back to whatever he came from."

Alice couldn't argue with that. Neverland was a nightmare compared to Wonderland, though she now found herself dealing with their people. She wondered for a moment if she should tell Peter what happened in Wonderland with so many of the Neverland people falling victim to the Queen of Hearts, then immediately decided against it. If he was telling stories, it was safer for her to not tell him anything he might be able to repeat.

"It's good of your dad to take him in," Heather said. "I don't know if I'd immediately send him away to school like this, but at least he's not wherever he used to be."

"Dad's travelling a lot again," Kevin said. "Ambassador and all, right? So he just isn't home enough to keep an eye on the kid. And Mom doesn't really like him that much. Mostly because his Korean's really bad. I honestly have no idea how he managed to find him in Korea and bring him home. Dad just asked me to keep an eye on him in case something came up."

"Looks like he's doing okay for himself so far," Heather noted, looking over at him. "You might not have to watch him too closely. Besides, we got our last year of middle school. Next year he'll have to fend for himself, so he might as well learn now."

Alice kept her eyes on Peter in the audience through the rest of the assembly. She couldn't get her mind around the fact that he was here in the first place. She might be able to shove him back through like she did with Cat and leave him there, but if he was part of Kevin's family now she might not be able to get rid of him.

At the very least, she needed to find out how he got here. Once she could be sure nothing else was following him, then she could go back to the original plan of just trying to get Adrianna's brothers back before the end of the year and falling to the Bandersnatch.

Unless she could somehow manage to get Peter to help her. She wasn't sure how flying would help, but she wasn't sure if he could do anything else on top of that. She really didn't know what to make of Peter just yet and she wasn't sure she really wanted his help, as great as it might be to have someone else helping her. Maybe he could even pick up whatever she couldn't finish after the Bandersnatch took her.

Alice knew it was a bad thing, but she resigned herself to the fate of the Bandersnatch. She didn't have any way to defeat it. There was nothing in the red book that could help her. The brown book was no longer in her possession. The green book...

She hadn't gone through the green book yet, but she somehow doubted there was anything useful in there to get rid of a creature like that. It looked like it was about plants, given the cover.

She needed to get back to transcribing that. Tonight, she would get back to looking through the books and creating her own database of useful terms before school started demanding more of her time. And when she was done, she would need to find someone to leave all of this research with so it wasn't completely lost when she disappeared.

CHAPTER 6

Book of Leaves and Curses

SCHOOL STARTED EXACTLY as Alice expected. There was little in the way of classwork that caused her any problems, most of this material covered by Ms. Miller in previous summers. Alice wondered when they would find something that Ms. Miller hadn't had the foresight to have already taught her, but for now she was grateful.

It left Alice with a lot of time to go through the books and make her notes. She left the red book aside for now, but she wasn't sure what to do with the green book now that she was looking through it. This one didn't fit with the documents she was working on at all.

Parts of the book looked like one of her biology textbooks. There were lists of plants, both things Alice had heard of and descriptions that made her think that some of them did not exist. She didn't know of any that would only glow blue in the light of a full moon, or something that would bloom with a seed on the third Sunday after watering it with the blood of your enemies. She wasn't even sure how someone would discover something like that.

There were so many plants and suggested combinations of them that would cause different results. There were potions for infatuation with a strong note saying that a love potion does not exist in the truest form, but infatuation is the closest you could ever get. There were obedience ones and ones to make people go blind and ones to sink people into deep sleeps that not even the most potent cures would be able to fix on their own. There were a lot of things to help people, but just as many that would cause harm.

And the plants were mostly very difficult to come by, if they existed at all. Alice was no gardener, but she was fairly certain that they didn't have access to most of these roots and specific animal parts that were required on the campus grounds. This book had nothing in it about trapping or anything like that, so it proved to be by and large completely useless to her in the hopes of her ever getting rid of the Bandersnatch with something inside of it. Unless she could find an enemy to draw enough blood out of to grow a sunflower on and water only in complete darkness until it was time to bloom.

"At least this one doesn't feel like people," Adrianna

offered late one night as she watched Alice work. The sun was only starting to set and Adrianna was busy on her own computer, sitting on her bed and going through some website or another that Alice wasn't on and that required her to follow things and people on it. Alice didn't get it, but Adrianna and everyone else seemed to like those things.

Alice nodded. It was a small thing, probably, but it didn't make her skin crawl touching it at least. She closed it for the night and she rose it into the air, it vanishing along with her arm as she put it back in its place. The ceiling above her bed should be impossible for anyone but her to get to without punching a hole in school property so it was the safest place she could manage on campus.

Her hand remained missing from her arm as her fingers crawled over the spines to another book, stopping at the one that felt like people. Her hand appeared holding the red book and she put it down on her desk without getting out of her seat. She opened it up, flipping through to the last page she was on and trying to find where she'd left off.

The lights flickered around them and went out. They could hear the panic happening around them in the other rooms, but Alice kept staring down at the book, only dimly lit by the glow of her laptop. Momentarily confused by the darkness, she turned back to Adrianna. Adrianna looked almost spooky, lit by the light of her screen, but just as confused as Alice felt.

"Power outage?" Alice asked.

Alice closed the book and put it back in its spot in the ceiling, picking up her computer and moving it around as a flashlight to try and figure out where she was supposed to be going. She looked around, trying to find something else that she could use that was less clunky than this. She probably had a flashlight in a bag somewhere, come to think of it. Before Alice could put down her computer, Adrianna picked up her cell phone and smiled at Alice.

"You really should ask your parents for a phone," she offered with a smile. "Then you'll have a flashlight for next time!"

A knock came at the door, Miss Amanda appearing there with a few candles in hand and wincing at the glare of Adrianna's flashlight. "Sorry," she said and Adrianna moved the light so it was no longer in her face. "Someone ran into a power line outside. Knocked out the power to the dorms. You're getting a few candles and you aren't to leave them lit overnight. When you go to sleep, the candles go out."

"Okay," Alice said, taking the candles from her. Miss Amanda went on to the next room to pass them along while Alice set up the candle at her desk, giving one to Adrianna, and setting the last one in the bathroom. She reached up and grabbed the green book out of the ceiling again before sitting back down at her desk. She was not about to start reading a book that felt like people by candlelight during a power outage. "I guess I can go through this one again. I..."

Alice blinked down at the pages, running her finger along the edge of the book and lifting to check the cover to make sure she'd pulled down the right one. It was the green book, but the pages looked completely different in the candlelight. The pictures were different, as well as the words. Even the handwriting scrawled across the pages.

"What is it?" Adrianna asked, peering over Alice's shoulder.

Alice moved the book out of the candlelight and towards the computer, the text changing back outside of the light of the flame. She moved it back in, finding the page was now covered in notes about how to use the plant if she could actually get her hands on it, as well as substitutes that she could use instead should some of them prove to be more difficult.

"There's something else here," Alice said, looking through the book. She reached backwards and pulled the red book out of the hiding spot, looking through it under the light as well. This one didn't have the same level of documentation in it that the green book did, but there were notes in the margins here and there, adding information to the books in the same handwriting. "Someone else wrote in these books."

Adrianna tried to look at the books, then soon backed away and found herself dizzy. She backed up, going to her own computer and made a disappointed noise as she declared they had no internet. Alice hadn't even noticed, not caring in light of these new notes, and ignored the bleeping of Adrianna's phone as she received several texts.

"Alice, have you seen Peter?" Adrianna asked.

"What?" Alice asked. "No. Not since the assembly. Why?"

"Apparently Kevin can't find him," she said, texting him back in the light of the small screen. "Sarah and Heather are going to help him look for him. You want to come help?"

"I won't be able to keep in touch," Alice said, not tearing her eyes away from the books. "You guys all have cell phones so you can call as soon as you find him. I'll stay here."

"Okay, call if he comes by here, then."

"Sure," Alice said, her eyes staying on the book as she started going through the side notes. She heard Adrianna leave and flipped through the pages, wondering what she could find in here and if she could use any of it to make something that would force the Case brothers to come back with her through the mirror before the Bandersnatch won. Or maybe something to give her more time.

There were a lot of things written in the green book,

the notes very thorough and many of them having nothing to do with the pages they were written on. While the book was largely about plants and potions and various ways to treat things or make other things go your way, the words in the candlelight were largely about revenge and getting the things you wanted or making people pay for causing you pain. The text was much more compelling, listing reasons that something might be used, but she didn't know why this wasn't written in the text. These notes were very specifically for the purpose of making people do things they would not otherwise do or making them pay for their disobedience. Innocuous side effects or no, Alice wondered just who this second author was in the book and what the first author had done to make him so mad.

She could hear people piling into the foyer, laughing and talking stretching up as far as her, but she stayed focused on her task at hand. Her window might have rattled, but the candle barely even flickered. She would get up to close that in a moment.

Her mind drifted back to the brown book, wondering if there were notes in there too. She might have been able to find a way to get rid of the Bandersnatch hidden in the margins if she'd known about this earlier. She wouldn't have to leave it all to chance, hoping she stumbled across something while only being able to prepare for the eventuality that something awful was going to happen. She wondered if she could let herself trade someone temporarily for the brown book and then get the person back as soon as she sent the Bandersnatch away.

The more she thought about it, the more she realized it was probably not a very safe bet. Counting on the fact that there were notes in the brown book at all, as well as hoping that the notes would actually outline how to get rid of the Bandersnatch, left too much to chance. She didn't have any guarantee that the book would have anything new, and she would just be losing a person to the Bandersnatch at that point. Unless she could find someone to trade for him to go away on his own. Was that an option?

"That's an evil face, Miss Wonderland."

Alice jumped out of her chair with a surprised yelp, landing hard on the ground from the sound of the intruder. She looked up, Peter floating there on the ceiling and looking down at her. He flew down further, getting his face right in hers and looking straight into her eyes. "Are you about to do something evil?"

"How did you…" Alice started, but she looked over to the open window and never finished. She didn't close it sooner and Peter had flown in. Of course he had. She was going to have to remember to close and lock that whenever Adrianna wasn't there, no matter how warm the room might get.

Peter floated away and placed his feet back on the ground,

bending over and looking at the books Alice was reading. He touched one cover and immediately jumped back. "Why do you have that?" he demanded, turning on her. "You can't have it! Those are evil! You're going to go evil if you read those! They don't have nice stories in them, Alice. You can't have them."

Alice sighed and got back up to her feet. "They're not that evil," Alice said. "I've been reading them and trying to figure out what's in them. They can help."

"Nothing in those books is going to help anyone." Peter backed away from them, though he looked like he wanted to tip the candle over and set them both on fire right then. His eyes kept flickering to Alice, waiting for some reason for him not to do it. Alice doubted that he understood anything about fire alarms, though she didn't know if they were working right now.

Alice shook her head and got back to her feet. She put the chair upright and picked up both books, putting them both back into hiding. "That's why Adrianna usually watches while I'm reading them," Alice told him. "She makes sure nothing happens to me when I read them. But look, all gone now. You don't have to worry about them anymore."

"You shouldn't have them," Peter said. "Those books need to be destroyed."

"You're overreacting," Alice told him. "I used to think that too, but they're just books. Books can't hurt you."

"You can't really say that," Peter said, shrinking away from her and looking scared. "*You*. You *know* what those books do. They're evil."

"The Queen of Hearts is still doing awful things without her book," Alice told him. "It's not the book that makes someone do bad things. The book just tells them how. If you don't want to do bad things, then you won't do bad things."

Peter shook his head. In a very small voice, he said, "She would never do those things if she never read the book." He looked back at her, almost pleading as he spoke. "You have to destroy it. Get rid of the book so you don't do the same thing. Get rid of all of them!"

"How did you even get here?" Alice asked, not wanting anything to do with the subject. "Weren't you in Wonderland the last time I saw you?"

Peter looked like a scared animal in the way he backed away from her, lit poorly by the candles. His gaze stayed on her for a very long time, shaking his head ever so slightly like she had suddenly grown two new, very dangerous heads. Alice made no move to come after him, watching him get closer to the window and his eyes finally left hers. They went behind her and he looked even more scared than before.

"It seems that she has finally found a little madness in that wretchedly dull place," the Cheshire Cat's silky voice said, drifting lazily through the air. He sounded very much like he did not want to be there at all. "Or perhaps she has only discovered her malice."

Alice turned back, looking into the wardrobe mirror and finding the Cheshire Cat in Tiger Lily's hand and pressed up against the glass. He slunk away, the room surrounded in a light smoke and Tiger Lily looking not at all ready to deal with him. She could see incense burning in the background and Adam was there, looking away like he was in the middle of a bad idea.

Behind them, the house was full of people. The bodies of several men, women, and a few that were neither at all were curled up on the ground. They all clutched their bloody, beating hearts in their hands, staring down at it longingly like they could not figure out what to do with it. There appeared to be very little room for them to walk. Adam perched on the back of a chair and shook his head while Tiger Lily stood in the foreground.

"Alice, we are in need of assistance," Tiger Lily said.

"I'm in the middle of something," Alice told her. "Can it wait?"

"What happened?" Adam asked. "Is Addie okay?"

"Power outage," Alice told him. "Addie's just helping

everyone else find Peter. Who is sitting in the corner and is very upset with me right now. Anyway, what did you need me for that it couldn't wait?"

"It has been a very long time since you came to us, Alice of Wonderland," Tiger Lily said. "We were unsure if you would ever return."

"She wouldn't just abandon us," Adam told her. "She just can't really get over here while she's at my place. But now that she's back at school, she'll come over more. At least, I assume this is where Alice was disappearing to back when I was still on her side."

"What's happening?" Alice asked again more sternly, trying to make this quick. "That's a lot more people than last time. Is the White Rabbit aware that you've filled his house with corpses?"

"These men still live," Tiger Lily said. "We are not so sure of the Mad Hatter. He has gone missing and the Tea Party still continues on without him."

"What?"

"The Mad Hatter's just dropped off the face of Wonderland," Adam told her. "There's nothing anywhere. No other tea parties, no sightings of people with outlandish hats, nothing. We can't find him anywhere and he was just starting on some big plan with the White King. Or he was supposed to tell us what the White King's plan was. He never made it back from that meeting. At first we thought he just got sidetracked."

"It has been too long, Alice of Wonderland," Tiger Lily told her. "We cannot wait any longer for him to return on his own. We must find him."

"So get the Cheshire Cat," Alice told her. "What makes you think I can find him? Cat's the one that finds people no matter where they've gone."

Cat squirmed against the mirror where Tiger Lily continued to hold him, letting out a threatening growl as he tried to struggle free of the grip she had on his scruff. "There was a time before today when I might have felt so inclined," he said, scratching at Tiger Lily's arm only for her to not flinch at the blood left behind from his scratch, "but I find myself less and less, shall we say, *compliant* by the day."

"You can't find him?" Alice asked. "How can *you* not find him? You're— Tiger Lily, can you put him down? I don't think he's going anywhere."

Tiger Lily let him go, Cat dropping to his feet in a purple huff and hissing at her, taking a swipe at Tiger Lily before he resettled in front of the mirror. "The Mad Hatter has chosen to not be found, though he should not be so difficult to find if you know where he is. Simply go there and you will find him. I have told this one the same thing, but she is even more rude and obstinate than you."

"So you have no idea where he is," Alice said, ignoring the jab. "Have you tried the Jabberwocky? He's always following Hatter around."

"I am not some dog, Alice dear," Cat said, warning in his tone. "Ask a dog and they will work harder. Ask a cat and they will demand a reason. Demand *from* a cat and you will bleed." He shot a glower back at Tiger Lily, who was brushing Adam's demands to see her arm off while she tended to the incense.

"I'll be over as soon as I can spare some time," Alice told him.

"Your spare time is coming very soon," Cat promised. There was a twinkle in his eye and a sneer in his smile that Alice knew all too well.

She felt the push behind her and knew before she landed what happened. Peter charged her from behind, pushing her through the mirror.

CHAPTER 7

Hunt for a Mirror

ALICE LANDED FACE first on a very small scullery maid, who curled protectively around the heart she held tight in her hands. Cat had slunk out of the way as soon as he saw her dive through, leaving her with a face full of another woman's back, though if the woman noticed Alice she did not show any sign of it. Alice turned herself over, finding the mirror only reflecting her own reflection and the room around her.

She let out a resigned sigh. "Peter," she muttered, getting back to her feet and putting her hand against the mirror. The cool glass against her fingers did not change as she tried to make it link back to the mirror she came out of. He broke the mirror after she went through, she knew. Because of course he did. Adrianna's mirror was also gone, as was the one in the washroom.

She still had until morning before anyone other than

Adrianna would notice her missing. Now that she was in Wonderland, she might as well stay and try to figure out what was going on with the Mad Hatter. It wasn't like she was going to get much else done with the books tonight.

Alice took a deep breath and the wave of dizziness hit her all at once. The world tilted and wavered around her as it hadn't a moment before. She stumbled and managed to catch herself, feeling that familiar and uncomfortable sensation of coming apart as the incense took hold of her brain and started to make her feel scattered. It was no wonder Cat wasn't quite himself when he spoke. She looked around, finding no doors or windows or anything open for him to run out of. She needed to open an *anything*.

She stayed on her feet, though swayed as she tried to get to get over to Tiger Lily and Adam. Her foot caught the legs of someone on the ground and she stumbled, kicking several people until she was down on the ground. Even down here, the world kept moving around her. She would almost welcome someone holding her upright or carrying her around, since it was getting far too difficult to stay upright on her own. She wondered if she should stop breathing so deeply, though her body didn't stop.

Tiger Lily pulled herself away from Adam and snatched up the incense. "You'll do better helping her right now," she snapped at him as she extinguished the smoke.

Adam went to Alice's side and tried to help her up to her feet. "Tiger Lily, can you open the door?" Adam asked, putting one of Alice's arms around his shoulders and walking her across the room. He maneuvered her around the bodies and dropped her down onto the couch, letting her put her head down between her knees as she tried to breathe deep until she was able to clear her head.

Alice could feel the gust of fresh air as the door swung open. The pitter patter of the Cheshire Cat's claws skittered across the floor as he made his escape, followed by no feet trying to stop him. She was tempted to join him, but not inclined to get up just now. A few deep breaths of incense had taken her more or less out, her head spinning as she tried to pull herself back together. Still, she could at least think straight this time, even if she couldn't quite stand properly.

"Did the Mad Hatter make it to the White King?" she asked, not raising her head from its spot between her knees.

"We don't have to do this right—"

"He did," Tiger Lily said. "He has gone missing since he returned with the message. I have been unable to find him and the Cat is unable to help."

"Was drugging him your first try?" Alice asked. "Because that generally doesn't work out that well."

"Asking nicely was the first thing," Adam told her. "Are you going to be okay?"

"As soon as I can breathe again," Alice told him. "What do you know about what happened to him? What was the message from the King? Where did he go missing?"

"We can wait a few minutes," Adam told her, ready to pull her back down if she tried to get up. Alice was very comfortable bent over and had no intention of any of that. "We don't have to do this right now."

"The message from the White King was simply that the Mad Hatter could do whatever it was that he was planning," Tiger Lily told her, shooting a glare at Adam.

"Tiger Lily! Give her a minute."

"Alice of Wonderland is much stronger than you believe," Tiger Lily said. "We do not know what he planned. He walked through the field of flowers with no faces. I believe that the Queen of Hearts found him and has enlisted him with no interest in whatever his plans may have been. She does not think that any force moving against her would exist."

"No, she wouldn't," Alice said, shaking her head and raising it up a little, closing her knees and staying hunched over as she tried to clear her lungs and head with more fresh air. "I hope she didn't, though. I don't know how we'd find his heart in the mess of them that she's already collected. I'd need to use him to actually find the right one."

"His plan was something to get all the hearts back," Adam said.

"The Mad Hatter's plan is unimportant," Tiger Lily told him. "The only thing that is important is that we find him once more. We have lost a valuable asset in the Jabberwocky. It has run away to the cliffs and refuses to return."

"It doesn't like me very much," Alice told her. "It's not coming back for me."

"That is why we need the Mad Hatter to return," Tiger Lily said. "It is too great a beast to lose to the Mad Hatter's disappearance. Adam and I are to try and gain the beast's favour, though it will be better suited to the Mad Hatter. It will listen to him."

"I'll see what I can find," Alice told her. "I can look for a little while tonight, but I need to go back before anyone notices I'm gone."

"So long as you have not forgotten your duty to us."

Alice kept her tongue still at that. She had no duty to them. She might feel *obligated* to help them, but Wonderland had caused her far more trouble for her than she thought she deserved. She knew that there were more than enough people there to solve Wonderland's problems, but there were other things that she actually needed to check.

"Have you seen Matt?" Alice asked. She looked up at Adam, trying to catch his eyes.

Adam looked away, refusing to meet hers. "Not yet," he said, sounding worried. "He's not in the forest, at least."

He glanced at Tiger Lily and didn't say anything more, though Alice understood his meaning. He hadn't gotten a chance to check Neverland yet because Tiger Lily wouldn't take him back. Alice was not sure how she felt about that, wanting to know but also not wanting Adam to get hurt while he was over here.

She hadn't felt anything in the back of her mind trying to get through the barrier, come to think of it, so maybe the refugees had stopped passing over. Or they were still pouring through and the sporadic pains and few moments of weirdness that happened now and then since last semester were caused by something else.

"You can continue to look for him after we retrieve the Mad Hatter," Tiger Lily said. "The Jabberwocky is too important to lose control of. Your brother is of no assistance."

Adam shot her a look of both anger and resignation. His mouth opened to speak, though he shut it again, his jaw clenched tight.

"All right," Alice said, getting to her feet. Her head felt clear enough and she was starting to feel better. "Let's see if I can track down the Hatter. If I find him, I'll send him back to the tea party, but I do need to go home sooner than later."

"Understood," Adam said. "Oh, have you had a chance to look into... this?" He waved his hand around the small house filled with unconscious bodies clutching their hearts.

"Not yet," Alice said. "I might have a lead, though. I'll let you know."

Adam nodded and left with Tiger Lily out the front door. Alice looked around and took a step over the body, appearing beside the White King's throne. The court bustled around her, men moving around and making themselves look important as they approached the King with their business, though the King was asleep on his throne. He set up in the ruins of the Duchess' castle, the castle slowly rebuilding itself around them. No one paid Alice any mind as she walked away from the throne room, through the castle, and out the front door.

She had to think of a way the Mad Hatter could have just gone missing. The man might have wandered off if there was something to distract him. There would be promise of something of a party somewhere, of people that he would want to talk to or a promise of something he might want to see, but he wouldn't have simply wandered off on his own without some sort of reason. It just might not have been a good one.

She kept thinking, trying to come up with something when another thought struck her. She could just see if she could find his hat. All she would need was the hat and she would be able to find the man who wore it. He was never without it after all.

She reached out and took hold of the hat, pulling herself along to where it currently rested. She felt the soft velvet under her fingers and it felt untouched, though Alice wasn't about to give herself too much hope. She might just be touching a fortunate part of his hat.

What she found when she came to the hat was a less promising. It sat alone in a small clearing where it looked like a table was just starting to come together under a circle of rocks and the remnants of a fire. She wasn't that far off the path and she could see it well enough from here, but the Hatter's hat was here with no owner. There was no sign of a struggle, thankfully, but there was only the very start of a tea party here as well. She had a feeling she knew what happened here.

Alice took the hat and looked down at her wrist, finding that she didn't have her watch on her for the moment. She wouldn't, what with the being pushed through the mirror, and she went instead directly back to the White Rabbit's house, finding it empty of anyone with their hearts in the right places. She needed to get back before anyone discovered she was missing and she wasn't sure how long she'd already been here.

Alice put the hat down on one of the people and stood in front of the mirror, trying to think of where she could come out. The mirror in her own room wasn't around anymore, nor was Adrianna's or the bathroom mirror. With those three main ones gone, she needed to think of another one that didn't have too many people around that she could conceivably just walk out of.

She checked Heather and Sarah's room next, knowing that they were out and looking for Peter the last time she was there. The candles were still lit in their room when she took a peek in, but there were people moving in it. It was definitely more than Sarah and Heather in there, and Alice changed it back to her own reflection before anyone could catch her looking in. Their bathroom would be just as suspicious, she knew, since people didn't just walk out of bathrooms before they entered the room in the first place.

The bathrooms downstairs were occupied as well. She couldn't check Kevin and Robert's room because she had never been there and had no idea where their mirror was. She considered trying Joe and Travis' room, but there was the problem of her being a middle school girl showing up in the high school dorms late at night in a boy's room. They would get in a lot of trouble if she did.

There was also the problem of using one of the school washrooms. They were empty, but she didn't want to be caught in the school after hours and get in trouble for it. Not again. Enough bad stuff had come from doing that by accident and she didn't plan to do it on purpose.

She needed an empty room in the middle school dorms somewhere. There was movement in every room she peered into, even in the dim candlelight, that she was running out of places that she could think to try. She went down a list of everyone she knew in those dorms, getting desperate until she finally figured out one room remaining.

Lance's old room appeared to be empty. If she moved quickly, she might be able to get in and out without anyone being the wiser. She just needed to get out of the mirror with no one looking over and she could go back to her own room and pretend like she never left. It didn't look like she'd been gone long.

With one last look, she went through the mirror, wondering if she had the right room. It still smelled weird, even with the candles, but it was completely empty of any sign of anyone living in here. Well, except for that sudden movement to her left.

CHAPTER 8

Ransacked

THE DOOR NEXT to her opened and she froze as some-one entered. Realizing she was caught if she stayed, she went back to the mirror and started to crawl back through to the White Rabbit's house. Maybe she could keep looking for the Mad Hatter for a couple more hours until morning.

Something grabbed her by the leg and dragged her out of the mirror. She let out a yelp of surprise, falling forward on top of Lance, who held onto her leg just a little too tightly. Behind her, Wonderland disappeared and she tried to get off of him.

"Alice!" he hissed at her as they untangled themselves. "Where the hell have you been?"

"Sorry," she said, getting up. "Peter pushed me in. I couldn't get back. I think something happened to the mirrors in our room. Why is your room so empty?"

"Everyone's trying to find you!" he said, dragging her out of the room and into the hall. She pulled herself free of him and let him escort her downstairs as he explained. "Addie's worried. Miss Amanda looks like she's about to put in martial law. I can't believe you would just pop over to Wonderland at a time like this!"

"Hey, I didn't mean for that to happen!" she snapped at him. "I was trying to tell Adam I was holding off on heading back there until the weekend. I didn't have time to do anything while I was over there anyway. And I don't normally let myself get trapped over there if I can help it! Why are you so mad?"

"When Addie got back to your room, it was completely trashed," he told her. "The mirrors are smashed and there's glass everywhere. It looks like someone went through and tore up everything they could get their hands on. And, of course, no one could find *you* anywhere."

"Everything?" Alice asked, going through everything in the room that she should check. She let one hand drift behind her back and felt along a few sections of the room. The hiding spot for the books was intact, her finger running over both spines just to be sure. At that, she breathed a sigh of relief. She needed to know that at least those two were safe. She had only just started to discover their secrets.

"It looked like everything," Lance said. "It's been almost

an hour since we started trying to find you. Everyone who knows what you look like is looking for you."

She went next to her computer, putting her hand on it and feeling something sharp cut into her finger. She pulled it back with a sharp intake of breath and put her finger in her mouth, tasting the metallic tang of her blood as her finger started to bleed.

"What the— What did you do?"

"Just wanted to see if everything was still there," Alice told him. "I think they got glass on my desk. But why was your room empty?"

"Alice, I don't live there anymore," he told her. "I moved to the high school dorms. I'm just here trying to help find you." He steered her into Heather and Sarah's room where Heather and Kevin sat with Adrianna and Miss Amanda. He let himself in, leading the way for Alice.

"Found her," Lance said. "She was wandering up on the fourth floor."

Adrianna, tears streaking her face, leapt at Alice and hung around her neck. Alice returned the hug awkwardly. Heather was there a moment later, watching her like everyone else, and Alice didn't know what to do with all the attention.

"Sorry," she said. "I got a little lost. I thought I'd come

and help you guys try to find Peter and I think I took a wrong turn. Lance said someone broke in?"

"Alice, you can't go wandering off like that," Miss Amanda said. "We were very worried. It's been an hour."

"I'll go get Rob and Sarah," Kevin said, excusing himself for the moment.

"I'm sorry," Alice said, trying to look as contrite as she could manage. This seemed to be enough for Miss Amanda, who softened and looked sympathetically at Alice.

"You girls are going to stay in here tonight," she said. "It looks like someone broke into your room while you were out and trashed the place. Do you remember if you locked the door before you left, Alice?"

The better question was if Adrianna locked it. She hadn't even thought to check that when Peter showed up and started talking to her, or even when Adam had appeared in the mirror. She had been getting far too comfortable with both of them, and she really should have checked the door. If someone had walked in during any of it, she would have been discovered and that would have been the end of everything.

"I don't think I did," Alice said, putting her hands in her pockets and not pulling out a key to the dorm room. Of course she wouldn't have it on her, but that should be enough to satisfy Miss Amanda from looking into it much more. She hoped that this whole thing would blow over fairly quickly.

"Okay," Miss Amanda said. "We'll deal with this more in the morning. You two come see me at ten tomorrow morning, okay? We'll get some spare blankets and mattresses for you both for now and you are both to stay out of your room until we get a better look at it in the morning, okay?"

Alice and Adrianna agreed, Miss Amanda leaving the three of them to their own devices.

"Seriously," Heather said once she was gone, "get a phone. All of this could have been solved if we could just text you to find out where you were."

"Sorry," Alice said again. "I just wanted to come help with looking for Peter. Did you ever end up finding him?"

Heather smiled and shook her head. "Oh yeah, we found him," she said. "He was in his room the whole time, apparently. Just hiding out in the corner and staring at the candle. He was looking like he'd seen a ghost or something, so we just left him there. And then Addie went back to your room and this whole mess happened."

"Sorry," Alice said. "I'll ask my parents if they can get me a phone for next semester."

"Why not just ask them tomorrow?" Adrianna asked.

"Tomorrow?"

"Miss Amanda said earlier that she was going to have to

call our parents in the morning anyway. You could always just ask when she does that and when she tells your parents about what happened. After everything that happened, they should say yes, right?"

Alice's heart fell. Her parents would not be happy to get a call from the school right now. They could barely handle being at a table together, much less deal with a call from the school about her. Alice found herself panicking anew, this time about how to get Miss Amanda to call off any attempts at a call home until Alice could figure out something else she could do to keep her parents from even thinking about her while they tried to navigate what remained of their marriage.

THOUGH SHE COULDN'T stop it, the call home was much better than Alice feared. Her mother answered and politely informed Miss Amanda that she should not be calling about Alice unless she had done something wrong. Miss Amanda didn't look happy about it, but Alice knew this was the best she could hope for.

Miss Amanda brought them back up to their room, their friends joining them in an offer to help them clean it up. At a glance, Alice could tell this was going to be much worse on her part than Adrianna's. While the whole room was covered in glass and papers, and even the bathroom vanity looked like it had been emptied and the contents thrown about, it was Alice's clothes and sheets that had been attacked. Her desk had been emptied of papers and her books were the ones on the ground. The whole room was trashed, but it was only Alice's stuff that had been touched.

"There is glass everywhere," Miss Amanda muttered, keeping them at the door. "Okay, we're going to find out just what is broken and we're going to be very careful. Get whatever you need out of here and maintenance will be by to fix it up a little later today, okay?"

Adrianna looked shaky, but Alice smiled at her and caught her around the shoulders, giving her a hug for support. "It's just some broken glass, right?" she asked.

"It's more than a little broken glass," Robert said peering in through the mass of people. Sarah next to him gave him a smack and he recoiled against it, saying nothing else after that and letting Alice and Adrianna go in. Alice stayed close to Adrianna as she collected her computer and a change of clothes for the day that she shoved in her untouched backpack.

Alice had a bit more trouble getting her stuff together. Her clothes were flung all over the place, a lot of it mixed in with the glass instead of neatly folded in a dresser that hadn't been touched. Her computer was on the desk covered in broken glass with the drawers ripped out and papers scattered across the room.

"I think someone had it out for you," Heather said quietly next to her, trying to help Alice find something in the mess that wasn't going to cut her when she picked it up. "It looks like they just tore apart your stuff. I'm not crazy, right?"

"Looks like," Alice said quietly back, but she didn't let herself get emotional about it. She was already pretty sure she knew what happened in here and she knew there was someone in particular who had a very specific agenda in going through her room right then. "Or maybe they heard someone coming and got out of here before they got to Adrianna's stuff."

Heather didn't look like she believed her, but she wasn't going to point out any of this to anyone else either. They had an understanding that Alice knew how to deal with her own matters and she wasn't going to get involved in things she didn't know much about. Not yet, anyway. This would have to happen again, and if it did Heather would not hold her tongue so readily.

Alice checked her suitcase in the bottom of the dresser where she kept some of her longer clothes for when the weather would get colder and managed to pull something out of there, leaving her computer under all the broken glass and abandoning it for now. The candle had fallen over on her desk and scorched a portion of the table before going out, but it looked like it had gone out before it had done much damage at least.

With clothes in hand and no desire to head to the washroom to see what could be recovered from there, they made their way back into Sarah and Heather's room to get changed. The boys waited for them outside until they were ready and they went to the cafeteria together.

"It looks like someone had the wrong room," Robert offered. "I mean, who'd go after either of you?"

Alice kept her face very still. She knew exactly who had gone after her and she was starting to feel the guilt build up in her for letting Adrianna get involved by virtue of being in the same room as her. When they were alone, she would try to explain.

"Maybe it was a jealous—"

"It is *never* a jealous lover, Sarah," Heather said. "Never."

"You don't *know* that," Sarah said. "For all we know, every night Alice might sneak out to see her secret boyfriend and he just got tired of the secrecy and decided to take revenge."

"Why are you saying that like it's supposed to be romantic?" Kevin asked.

"You just don't know romance."

"Why am *I* always the one with the secret boyfriend?" Alice asked.

"Because *you* might actually be able to keep it secret," Sarah said. She kept her tone light, but Alice wondered if there was something else there. Sarah had been taken by the

Bandersnatch and Evan remembered everything. She wondered how much Sarah remembered, and if she remembered that Alice had failed to save her.

If she did, Sarah did not let on. If she did remember, maybe she was comfortable just accepting the new memories that the Bandersnatch put in place. At least, she wasn't trying to pull Alice aside and demand to know what happened to her. Nothing was bothering her much right now.

If anyone looked concerned about the break in, it was Adrianna. Her room had been invaded and she didn't have the benefit of knowing that the culprit wasn't after her yet. Alice needed to tell her and that she didn't need to worry about it happening again. Probably not, anyway.

"So what exactly happened, anyway?" Alice asked instead. She wanted to know what other people thought had happened. "I mean, I left to find you guys and when I get back there's all this happening."

"We were looking for Peter and it looked like we weren't going to be able to find him anywhere when Robert decides to just go back and check Pete's room again," Kevin told him. "He's just sitting there in a corner staring at a candle on the floor. I swear he wasn't there when we checked before, but he's looking pale so I stuck around with him for a bit until he calmed down. Never said what he saw, but... He does that sometimes."

Alice could think of what he saw and what he did to make him end up like that, but she kept her face blank and cocked her head sideways. "Okay, so he wasn't really missing," she said. "So what about the room?"

Sarah chimed in. "Well, since Peter was found, we headed back down and ran into Mi... Lance? He was coming down to check on Adrianna, but he's looking a little panicked and he says that someone broke into your room while we were out and when we go to see it for ourselves, it's just wrecked. We called Miss Amanda right away and we had to try and find you after that because, well, room's a mess and you aren't even there for it. You could have gotten kidnapped or something."

Or something. Alice kept her face neutral as she took it all in, nodding along and making her plans to slip away and find Peter as soon as she could. She had no idea what she was going to do to make him stop, or if he even knew that she was back in the first place, but she was going to have to confront him at some point about all of this. He was much more of a nuisance than Cat already. At least he never wrecked her room or brought Adrianna into it.

Except for the times he did.

Alice needed to get something that kept Wonderland and Neverland people to leave her room alone. That would be the next thing she looked up in the book. Something to keep people from other worlds from entering her room and making trouble for her. The green book in the candlelight might have something for that.

"You sure you didn't want to at least grab your computer out of your room?" Kevin asked.

Alice shook her head. "There was way too much glass. I might just go grab a book out of the library if I need to do something."

Heather gave her a look at that, but very carefully said nothing. Alice could tell she wanted to make a big deal out of the fact that it was only Alice's side of the room, but she wouldn't.

Adrianna had finally started to calm down a little more from her frazzled state and was relaxed as they got food and sat down. They stopped talking about what happened in the room and found other things to be distracted by. They talked about classes and electives and how they only had a year left of middle school.

Alice relaxed and said little, giving herself enough room to let everyone else do their thing to make it all go away. Soon enough, they would be able to head back to the dorms and do something to waste a little time until both Alice and Adrianna could go back to their room and everyone could forget this happened.

As it was, they were getting strange looks and whispers. It was easy for everyone to figure out what happened, but she was sure the fallout for this was going to be a pain. Miss Amanda would want to find out who did it and make them pay for what they did, but there would be no way for them to prove it. People were already talking among themselves about the girls who had their room trashed. While Alice could deal with it, she worried that Adrianna wouldn't be able to handle that kind of attention.

She'd have to teach her what to do. She just had to pretend none of it bothered her and people would eventually get bored and leave her alone. All they needed to do was wait for the whole thing to blow over and it would be fine.

Part way through the food, Adrianna got a text and looked down at her phone. When she looked up, she was apologetic. "Joe wants to see us," she told Alice. "I think he heard about what happened. I told him we're fine."

Alice shrugged and looked around. "I guess we're going. See you back at the dorms a bit later?"

"You want us to come with?" Kevin offered.

"We should be fine. Thanks."

The pair of them excused themselves and made their way outside, Alice glad for a moment with Adrianna without everyone else around. "I'm sorry," she started not knowing what else to say to start.

"About what?" Adrianna asked. "You aren't the one that broke into the room and broke everything."

"It's my fault though," Alice told her. "Have I told you who Peter is?"

"Kevin's brother?"

"He's also Peter from Neverland," Alice told her. "I don't know how, but he made it over here and became Kevin's brother. He came by after you left and he got a little freaked out by the books. I don't remember if I told you, but there was a black one that showed up in Neverland and drove one of his friends crazy and created all the zombies that are all over the place there. When he saw I was reading the books, he got kind of weird and he pushed me into Wonderland."

"Can he do that?" Adrianna asked.

"Apparently. Tiger Lily wanted to talk about some stuff. Wonderland is a whole different thing, but after he pushed me in. I think he broke the mirrors so that I couldn't get back out. I turned around as soon as I got to the other side and the mirror to get back was gone. Every mirror in the room was just gone."

"How did you get back?"

"I had to use Lance's mirror to get back through," she said. "He didn't look that happy about it, but every other one I tried had people around and I can't explain crawling out of a mirror."

"At least you got back okay," she said. "And it didn't take you too long! Sometimes you end up in Wonderland for days when you get pushed in, right? So at least you got back out pretty quick. Maybe Wonderland is learning to deal with things on its own without needing you to stick around so much."

Alice smiled, but her eye was drawn by movement flickering across campus. Peter. "Can you meet with Joe on your own?" she asked, keeping an eye on him so she didn't lose him. "You can make it the rest of the way on your own, right?"

"Yeah, but where are you going?" she asked. "He said he wanted to see both of us. I think he just wants to make sure we're okay so he has something to tell your sister about everything and make sure for her that you're okay too."

"I can email her tonight," Alice told Adrianna. "I need to talk to Peter about last night right now."

Alice nodded across campus to where Peter was talking to a group of people in his class and Adrianna seemed to understand. "Okay," Adrianna said. "I'll tell him you're okay for you."

"Thanks," Alice said. She looked around and was gone a moment later when they walked around the corner.

Alice appeared on the other side of the field, stepping out from behind the tree and trying to catch Peter's eye from the other side of the pond. His friends were sitting with him on the other side and he looked surprisingly fine for someone who was apparently traumatized last night after trashing her room.

Peter met her eyes and went white. Alice assumed he hadn't heard about her return just yet, and he froze on the other side of the pond. Alice quickly nodded into the forest and stepped back behind the tree, coming out behind another one just inside the treeline. She didn't want to have to do this around his friends if she didn't have to.

She didn't have to wait long before he came into the forest to meet her, soaring into the treetops. He stayed a good ways away from her, perched in a tree and staring her down. She stayed relaxed and went closer to him so that he didn't have to yell. She didn't want their conversation to be heard from the campus.

"You really didn't think that was going to work, did you?" she asked.

"I thought it would slow you down a little," he admitted. "I mean, how was I supposed to know that you would come back? Can you do that with every mirror here? I thought it was only special ones."

"Peter, can you please not try to keep me in Wonderland?" she asked. "I have a whole life here. I am just trying to keep everything here in order without messing it up and you're making it really hard to keep a low profile by destroying things."

"But you should be over there," he insisted. "You can save Wonderland. And then you can save Neverland. And then when you're all done with that, you can come back and just pick up where you left off."

"That's not how it works," Alice told him. She let out a deep sigh and realized she couldn't actually get mad at him. He was a child and thought that what he was doing wasn't nearly as bad as what she assumed. "Time passes in Wonderland and time passes here. If I'm gone for too long, people notice."

"Can't you just go over there and fix everything anyway? I saw Tiger Lily and that place with all the sleeping people. They were holding… things. It looked like something you knew how to deal with, so shouldn't you just go do that?"

"Shouldn't *you*?" Alice asked. "They're *your* people." She let out a sigh. "I don't know how to fix them yet. I need to keep going through the red book and try to figure out something in there to make it all work like it did for the people in Wonderland. I don't know why it's different in Neverland, but clearly there's some difference there."

"Those were all people from Neverland?" Peter asked. He looked and sounded very small in that moment.

"Yeah," Alice said. "The Queen of Hearts wants to take over Neverland. She's trying to take everyone's hearts to make them loyal to her, but no one in Neverland seems that willing to give theirs up. It's going to take a bit for me to figure out how to make their hearts go back in."

"And you need to read the book to find out how?" Peter asked. He sounded terrified.

"Yeah," Alice said. "I do. And that's why I need you to not try to keep me in Wonderland and I need you to stay away from the books. I am not going to be able to save anything if I can't figure out how and all the answers are in those books. If you want me to save Neverland for you, I need to be able to study those books and come back to keep reading them. Because I can't keep those books over there. You've seen the damage they cause when they do that. If they stay over here, then they aren't dangerous and they aren't going to make anything over there any worse."

"But they're evil," Peter said. "You're going to turn evil if you read them too."

Alice shook her head. "I haven't turned evil yet," she said. "Besides, if I don't read them, I'll never be able to save anyone. Not even that friend of yours. So you're going to have to let me keep going. So no more breaking in and trashing my room, okay?"

Peter looked hesitant, like he was preparing for a way out of the deal, but he couldn't think of anything to get around it. "I guess," he said finally. "If you really want to save Neverland for me. I was going to make John save it for me instead, but I guess I can let you do it."

Alice let out a sigh and shook her head. It was as good as she was going to get out of him and she would take it.

CHAPTER 9

Back to Normal

THEIR ROOM WAS cleaned up a day later and Alice was glad to put it all behind her and fall back into her usual routine. The pattern of school, work, and her days spent in the library were familiar and comforting. They were soon busy enough that they didn't notice the hours passing and Alice was glad for the normalcy.

The only new thing was their company. Where before it had only been the six of them, there was a new face that started to show up every night at their study table. Peter lingered at a table nearby with his own friends, casting glances their way as well as loudly talking about all the things he could do if he really wanted to. It wasn't so bad, but she could see Kevin shaking his head when Peter spoke too loudly. Everyone else with a sibling at the table was sympathetic.

"It's just what they do," Robert told him. "You realize

what a pain in the ass you were for whoever's older than you watching the younger ones. Although, I don't think anyone is as much of a pain in the ass as my older brother..."

"No one is as big of an ass as Terry," Heather assured Robert. "No one."

"He still causing problems?"

Heather shook her head and she rolled her eyes, debating in her head how much she wanted to rant about it. "He decided to show up for the first meeting of the year," he said. "He decides to pick a fight with Tasha. *Again.* And she kicks his ass. *Again.* And he just keeps being an asshole the whole time. He won't leave. Apparently there's something your dad is working on to make it so that we have to let him back in or something? It sounds like bullshit to me."

"It is," Robert told her. "He tried to make Dad do something about it over the summer. Dad said he would just to shut him up, but when it was time to deliver, he pulled out and told Terry he had to learn a thing or two about politics and he'd have to deal with this one himself. Dad wants him to drop the whole thing because his grades are crap and he isn't going to be able to get into university if he keeps going after Tasha instead of studying."

"You mean the club."

"No, I mean Tasha," Robert told her. "She turned him down ages ago and he hasn't gotten over it."

"He told you this?"

Robert got a look on his face as if he'd said the wrong thing and made a very long sound. He ended it with a nervous laugh and looked back down at the homework. "So anyone got question six?" he asked. "I'm getting three hundred and twelve and that doesn't look right somehow."

"Three hundred fifteen," Alice said absently. She should probably tell Tasha that they found Lori as well, though she was pretty sure that Travis would take care of that. He should, at least. Alice barely knew Tasha, despite how interested the older girl seemed in her last time they met, and she suspected as soon as Tasha found out that Lori was safe and well, she wouldn't want anything to do with Alice anymore.

"Any luck about getting your parents to let you join, Alice?" Heather asked. "It would be awesome to have at least one other girl from our year in there. No one else seems to want to and Terry's making everything such a pain in the ass these days."

"Just kick him out," Robert said. "He can't do shit about it."

"You going to share whatever you've got on him, then?" Heather asked, eyebrow raised. "Big bro seems to have more than a few things on you as well, you know."

Robert fell silent again, mouth open like he might say something more but not wanting to draw any more attention to himself from that and letting them talk around him. Alice smiled at him and shook her head. Anything more said at this point was probably just going to get him in trouble.

"Someone giving you problems?" Peter asked. He'd been hovering behind Kevin, holding his homework with a question now forgotten. His eyes darted between Heather and Robert, trying to figure out what was going on, positive that it was more interesting than the paper in hands.

Kevin shook his head. "Nothing you need to worry about, Pete," he said, moving his hand and gesturing for Peter's homework. "What's the problem?"

"Oh, it's this thing," Peter said, pointing out the problem on the page, his eyes glancing back at Alice as she drifted back to her own homework while Heather leaned over to keep talking to her.

"Seriously, Alice. Join. I need another girl and I have a feeling you're my best bet."

"My parents won't let me join," Alice told her. "Even if I could, didn't Terry say that this had something to do with Lori too? He was making a deal out of it when I was there last time. I don't want to be dragged into all of this if I don't have to."

"I don't remember that," Heather said. "Look, Tasha's got your back, even if he's got a problem with you. Come on."

"No permission form," Alice said. "You know the rule."

"Screw the permission form," Heather said. "You need it."

"Need it?" Robert asked. "Why would she need it?"

Heather shot Alice a look, the same one on that day they saw her room trashed. Heather still thought that Alice had attracted more trouble than she could deal with. She had been paying far too much attention all this time to the number of times Alice had tried to cover up the little injuries she had gotten or tried to hide in the name of covering up her voyages to Wonderland and the things she'd done to try and keep herself sane between the two places.

"It's good for anyone to know," Heather said simply. "You could probably do with a bit of self-defence yourself. If you aren't careful, Terry might get pissed off at you next and I am not going to be there to punch his douchebag lights out."

"You got some guy you need taken care of?" Peter asked, puffing up and looking across the table away from Kevin.

"Pete, don't—"

"I don't care how tough this guy is," Peter said, looking proud of himself and a little too full of himself as well. "I can take down a *pirate* so I don't think anything can stop me."

"What about zombies?" Alice said quietly, looking at him sidelong as her body shifted back down to her homework.

Peter went still, though Kevin was the only one who noticed it. He looked between Peter and Alice, but did not have time to place what was going on before Heather grinned and leaned forward.

"Pirates, huh?" she asked, the grin firm on her face and akin to what she'd seen on Lance's face before he went off and caused problems. "Well, if you think you can take Robert's big brother, then you should come by Combat Club at some point this week. He's been giving us a lot of trouble."

"I think I can do that."

"You are not picking a fight with a guy twice your size, Pete," Kevin snapped at him, shooting a warning look at Heather. "Don't encourage him."

"The bigger they are," Peter said, smiling as he took his homework back from Kevin. He was almost skipping back to his seat. Alice didn't have a doubt that he would show up and she was more worried for what he might try to do. Peter was not subtle.

"Heather, what were you thinking?" Kevin demanded of her. "I'm going to need to watch him like a hawk to make sure he doesn't get into anything now."

Heather laughed and shook her head. "Tasha would never let him do it," she told him comfortingly. "But if you need him to get a bit less out there, it might do him a bit of good. And you got a musical to train for this year, right? So you can't be keeping an eye on him constantly."

"The same musical *you're* doing," Kevin said. "I don't care how minor a role you got this year, you are going to be too busy with all your crap to keep an eye on him either."

"Calm down, Kevin," Robert said. "You can't keep an eye on him all the time and keep him out of trouble. It'll be fine."

Kevin remained in a sour mood the rest of the evening, even when Sarah and Adrianna joined them from their choir practice. Alice took the moment to excuse herself back upstairs to get her computer, wanting a break from everyone for just a moment, though mostly Heather. Now that it was in her head again, she kept prodding her about Combat Club.

Unfortunately, Heather followed her up, catching her by the shoulder and falling in step beside her as they went up the stairs. They were silent on the way up and down the hall, though Alice was sure it wouldn't last for long.

"Are you sure you can't convince your parents to let you join?" Heather asked.

"Maybe next year," Alice said. "I can ask my mother after they settle everything."

It would also be when Alice wasn't going to be around anymore. The Bandersnatch would have claimed her by then, so Heather wouldn't have to worry about her. She should see if Sarah still remembered that Alice had agreed to let her set her up on a date. She could postpone that for next year as well so that she wouldn't have to deal with that either.

"Settle?"

"They've been arguing a lot lately," Alice told her. "I'm pretty sure they'll actually file the whole way for divorce this time."

"Oh Alice," Heather said, suddenly sounding very sympathetic. "I'm so sorry."

"Once they do, my mother might be willing to sign the form for me, though," she said. "Lori said, anyway. She seems to think our mother is a lot more reasonable."

"Are you sure you're okay?" Heather asked. "I mean, you're taking this weirdly well."

Alice shrugged, unlocking the door and letting them both into her dorm. "It's probably for the best," she said. "They've been having trouble for a while. And then there was the stuff with Lori. They kicked her out and our mother hasn't been that happy since that happened. Or before. I don't think they're going to get along for much longer. Lori said this time it's her fault instead of mine, though. Huh."

Alice stopped inside the door, far enough for Heather to come in, and she looked at her wardrobe door. It was open, her suitcase knocked out of place to keep it that way. She tried to kick the suitcase back in, but something had fallen in the way to keep the suitcase in place. She knelt down and started to shuffle everything back around in the bottom of her wardrobe.

"Alice?" Heather asked. "Everything okay?"

Alice opened the suitcase and went through the contents to make sure everything was where it was supposed to be. It looked like someone had gone through it, but they hadn't taken anything out. Nothing, as near as she could tell, was missing.

"Alice."

"It's nothing," she told Heather. One last zipper to check.

"Then why are you going through your bag?"

"It's nothing."

"Don't bullshit me, Alice. What's going on?" she demanded. Heather stood behind her as Alice zipped her suitcase back up and put it back. "You didn't leave the closet open, did you? Someone's been in here."

"Nothing's missing," Alice said, closing the wardrobe. She looked at the bed and pushed the mattress back in place with her knee, more bothered that someone had moved it than that they had gone through clothes she hadn't worn since she got to school. She looked around and tried to figure out what else was altered. She found only the open window.

"So someone broke in here again?" Heather asked. "Alice, you have to tell Miss Amanda. There's something going on here."

"It's nothing," Alice said, glancing back at the mirror. Good, no sign of Wonderland. Heather was getting too curious and observant already. She couldn't deal with her seeing that now as well, but just in case Alice locked out any access in or out of Wonderland. She glared at the mirrors one final time as she crossed the room to the window, closing and locking it.

Heather stepped between her and the computer on her desk. "Come on, Alice," she said. "What's going on? It's obviously something."

"It's nothing," Alice said. "Adrianna was probably just looking for something. We get our stuff mixed up all the time in here."

Heather leveled a stare at her. "This room is immaculate," she told her. "There's no way. Look, at the start of the year your room gets broken into, all the mirrors are smashed and the whole place is torn up, but it's just *your* stuff that gets thrown around. And now things are just a little out of place? That's weird. You know that's weird and you being so calm about it makes me think you know something."

"Who else would it be?" Alice asked. "The door was locked. Miss Amanda and Adrianna are the only ones with a key to it. Do you really think either of them is going to do anything to me? And remember, I didn't lock the door at the start of the year. Who's going to coincidentally try the door, happen to find the room empty and decide to just wreck *my* stuff?"

Heather faltered at that. "You're coming with me to Combat Club this week," Heather said at last, stepping aside and letting Alice get her computer. "I will drag you if I have to. You are coming."

"Okay," Alice said, grabbing her computer and walking past Heather out of the room. She really should go this week anyway. She needed to make sure Peter didn't try anything when he decided to show up. And now she'd need to straighten him out again over breaking into her room a second time. She'd have to try to remind him that she needed those books, whether he liked them or not.

CHAPTER 10

Combat Club Rumble

ALICE WENT WILLINGLY with Heather to the next Combat Club meeting, though she had no intention of learning anything while she was there. She still had no permission slip, and no amount of her wanting it was going to change that. But she would watch everything she needed to. Including the other spectators.

Already there and looking around was Peter. He looked even more like a pixie child when he was wearing his normal clothes, the boy clearly not hearing about the athletic clothing requirement for the club. She was glad to have caught him and she was put on the bleachers by Heather, who immediately went to Peter's side and brought him over to Tasha.

From her body language, she could already tell that Tasha was unimpressed with Peter's talk, but more than willing to let him have a shot. He seemed to already think he was too good for some of the options, shaking his head as she pointed out the specialties and being very direct about what he was interested in. Heather said something in the mix of things and Alice just watched as Peter seemed to give in to whatever teasing she offered.

He looked around and caught Alice's eye as she sat in the bleachers. She nodded at him and made no move to do anything else, Peter looking a lot more hesitant to do much else as Tasha started to walk him around the gym and get him better acquainted with it.

Tasha spotted Alice in the bleachers and waved her down. Alice reluctantly got up from her seat, Tasha smiling broadly at her and sending Heather off to run laps with everyone else while she kept Peter at one side and keeping her other open for Alice.

"Alice, I was hoping that Heather would bring you around," she said. "Guessing your parents still said no?"

Alice shrugged. "Maybe next year?"

Tasha looked sympathetically down at her. "Maybe you don't ask your dad," she said, the smile looking forced. "He had some rather strong words for the club that he found out his dear sweet daughter was going to try and join, if I remember right. Don't really want to deal with any more of that if you try to push it any further."

"Sorry," Alice said quickly. She could feel Peter watching

the exchange, confusion across his face as he didn't understand what was going on.

"I hear you found Lori," Tasha offered instead. "Where's she been holed up the past two years?"

"She's been living at Adrianna's house," Alice told her. "Case. She's working for her mom and going to public school over there now."

Tasha's smile grew very tight and she blinked very slowly down at Alice. "She's been at the Case's this whole time." She nodded, looking at a loss for words and her eyes glancing at any moving person that came too close on their laps like she was looking for something to take some aggression out on. "Of course she has. Oh, those two aren't going to be able to walk straight for a month when I get through with them."

"She said she didn't want to be found," Alice offered. "I wasn't even supposed to find out."

"Doesn't matter, still going to beat them up." Tasha's smile returned to being light and she offered Peter to Alice. "Can you keep an eye on this one?" she asked. "No slip, no training. But he's more than welcome to watch and I'll be around for questions."

"Sure," Alice said, gripping Peter by the shoulder and directing him to the bleachers. Keeping an eye on him was exactly what she had planned anyway.

"What was that?" Peter asked, incredulous and confused

at the exchange. At the very least, Kevin had managed to teach him to be quiet during conversations he didn't understand that had nothing to do with him. "You have to actually *listen* to your parents? Don't they know who you *are?*"

Alice shook her head and forced him to sit down. "I'm not anything out here, Peter," she said. "I'm just Alice, ordinary student who isn't allowed to learn anything about fighting outside of whatever they teach in gym class. And you are Peter, ordinary student who can't fly and who needs to stop going through my room."

"But I *can* fly," he said. "And you can disappear and you save Wonderland."

"There is no Wonderland here," Alice said firmly, keeping her voice much lower than Peter's was. "There is no Neverland. There is only Lucena Academy and the rest of the world. There is no magic, no fantastic creatures, no big dangers that you need to fight, and you really should just imagine there are also no books out here that you're scared of."

"But the books are real."

"Forget about them," Alice insisted. "The books aren't your problem. Just try to be normal while you're here. Or, if you have to continue acting like this is Neverland, at least don't try to drag me into it. I'm already dealing with enough stuff without having to worry about you on top of it all."

"You're kind of bossy," Peter sad, crossing his arms next

to her and leaning back in the bleachers against the next set of seats. "Maybe I won't *let* you save Neverland after all. You might take all the credit."

Alice let it drop at that, watching as the people around them on the mats started to pair up and get to work on some basics. They weren't bringing out the equipment just yet. Instead they were going around in stations learning various hand to hand techniques, working slowly through several styles and ways to do various different holds, punches, and grapples.

She couldn't help but feel like all this would be very useful, though reminded herself she only had a year left to worry about it if she didn't find a solution for the Bandersnatch. And she didn't have time for that with everything else she had to do. She really should start working through the curses in the green book. Maybe she could slip away early tonight to go through it for something useful.

"Wait a minute!" Peter said after a moment of watching. "I didn't go looking for your stupid evil books."

Alice looked at him and tried to figure out why he was bothering. "The window was open and my stuff was moved around," she said. "Who else is getting into my room through an open window?"

"Anyone else who can fly," Peter said as if it were the most obvious thing in the world.

"So you," she said. "No one else flies. Anywhere."

"What about someone who can do the disappearing thing you do?"

Alice shook her head no.

"This place is so *boring*," Peter said. "And I don't want anything to do with those books. They're evil. You should destroy them before they make you evil too."

"You should stop trying to find them and destroy them for me," she said. "You won't find where they're hidden anyway. You've already tried to tear the room apart once trying to find it."

"No I didn't," he said. "When did I try?"

"Right after you broke all the mirrors in the room," Alice reminded him. "You tore apart my side of the room after that. *Just* my side of it. You didn't even touch Adrianna's, so you were obviously looking for something of mine in there somewhere."

Peter shook his head, but this time he shrank when he did it. "No," he said. "I just broke the mirrors so you would go over there and save everyone and not come back until you did. There was someone else who came in and was looking for stuff."

"Really." Alice didn't believe him for a moment, keeping her eyes on all the stations as Tasha walked around, correcting people here and there.

"I think he was one of the Lost Boys that Wendy made," he said. "He moved like them. He came in and he started doing something, so I left before he saw me. I could have beaten him up, of course," he added, getting his backbone back and straightening up more as he talked, "but I didn't want to get in trouble for being in a girl's room when it was dark. Kevin doesn't want me to be getting in too much trouble, and since he asked so nice, I thought I'd be nice back."

"How *kind* of you," Alice said flatly. She doubted Peter saw anything in her room at all, probably just trying not to get in more trouble from the fact that he definitely destroyed her room and got caught. He was probably still looking for the books and he would try to be subtle about it now. If he could be subtle. Still, she wasn't about to let him get away with it if he did it again. She would have to figure out what she could do to someone else's younger brother.

She could turn him in. That would make Heather get off her back, at least. Kevin would be upset with Peter, but it was obvious that there was something strange about him already. She could just tell everyone that Peter was the one going in and moving all of her stuff around. Maybe that would be enough to make him stop, and then he would be watched while she would be able to actually work.

She needed to figure out how to get the hearts back. She needed to have something to try in Wonderland soon and she had to see how Adam and Tiger Lily were doing with the Jabberwocky while she was gone. Though the White Rabbit's house was filling, Tiger Lily and Adam were not always there when she checked in on the other side.

Alice found herself almost hoping the end of the school year would come faster. The Bandersnatch taking her away would be much more peaceful than all of this.

The doors next to the bleachers slammed open and Alice could feel the douchebag emanate off the boy who entered. Terry was just as big of an asshole as she remembered from the last time he was here, dressed in his school uniform instead of gym clothes and looking around for Tasha.

Alice bristled at the sight of him, not sure what it was about him that made her dislike him so much. Maybe it was just the fact that he was mean to Tasha, who had been nothing but kind to her. Or the fact that Robert seemed to share a hatred of him when he could form no feelings that strong for anyone else.

"Is that Terry?" Peter asked, looking over at him. "He doesn't look that big."

"No one ever said he was big," Alice said. She noted that, given Peter's slight frame, Terry was actually twice his size, but she made no comment. "He's just a pain. He likes to make a lot of trouble for people who don't deserve it."

A smile played on Peter's lips. "He doesn't look that big," he repeated, getting up.

Alice grabbed him by the arm out of habit, but found herself hesitating in trying to keep him there with her. Peter was causing her problems. Terry was causing Tasha problems. She didn't like either of them right now and she would be a lot better off if the two of them took one another out.

"No flying," she told Peter quietly.

He smiled broadly back at her, wider and more genuine than she'd ever seen from him. "I'll take it as a challenge," he said. "This is going to be *so* easy."

Alice was going to get in so much trouble from Kevin, but she didn't care right now. Peter left her open hand and walked over to Terry with a definite spring in his step, though both feet were definitely hitting the ground. She moved closer, staying on the bleachers and looking over the edge to see the confrontation.

"Permission slip check!" Peter said to Terry, getting right in his way so he couldn't get any closer. "You can't join unless you have a permission slip, you know. Very mandatory."

"Out of my way, kid," Terry said, moving to push him out of the way.

Peter ducked under his arm and stayed firmly in his path. The smile on his face didn't falter. "I'm sorry, but if you don't have a permission slip, you have to go to the bleachers instead of the mats. It's the rules. You know how it is. So, permission slip?"

"Get out of my damn way!" he said, trying to push Peter aside again. Peter again sidestepped his attempted grab and shove, moving too quickly for him to catch. Alice kept an eye on Peter's feet, making sure they stayed on the ground, and found that he was being very true to his word. No flying. It was just that he was naturally that annoying.

"You *do* need a permission slip," Peter insisted. Behind him, he was starting to get some attention, with a few people moving in closer and Tasha storming over. No one intervened or said anything to stop them. As far as what had actually happened so far, neither had laid a hand on the other and Tasha wanted to be there to stop it before that happened.

"I don't need to show you a damn permission slip!" Terry yelled at him, grabbing his shoulder bag by the handle and swinging it down at Peter.

"That's *enough!*" Tasha roared, running to their side to see Peter, who looked like he must have been hit in the scuffle. Alice knew better.

Peter popped up behind Terry, tapping him on the back. "So are you saying you don't have a slip?" Peter asked again, continuing to dodge the wide blows that Terry kept throwing his way. Peter was laughing as he weaved around Terry, appearing a moment later after dodging each blow, having just missed it or manoeuvred around Terry entirely.

Tasha got there and grabbed Terry by the bag arm and twisting it behind him until he was down on one knee. "I don't know how many more times I have to tell you this," Tasha said, her voice not quiet but the rest of the gym silent fell as she spoke, making it sound like it was booming, "but get the hell out of here. You were banned for a damn reason and picking a fight with non-members is just another reason to keep you out."

"You can't prove a damn thing," he said through clenched teeth.

"Actually," Heather said from the back, one of several people with cellphones in their hands recording the scuffle, "I'm pretty sure this will hold up in a court of law as you attacking Peter. I'm pretty sure your dad won't be too happy to see these floating around online either."

Tasha smiled back at her and, with Terry defeated, she let go of him. He got back to his feet, brushing himself off and picking up his bag. He leaned in close, though Alice didn't hear what he said to Tasha before he finally left the building.

"I thought I told you to stay on the bleachers," Tasha said with a grin at Peter. She gave him a smack on the arm for his work. "Nice moves, though. I don't think we have anyone who moves like that here. Hope you show up to the tryouts next week."

Peter looked pleased with himself when he got back to the bleachers. "And I didn't have to fly once," he told Alice, leaning back against the bleachers and looking positively pleased with himself.

Alice wasn't paying attention to him anymore and Peter looked down at the book in her lap to see why. He jumped away from her out of fear, seeing that Alice had placed the red book inside her math book and started reading through all of it.

"What?" Alice asked without looking up at him. "You wanted me to save Neverland, right? I need to figure out how to make this damn spell work for people from Neverland."

CHAPTER 11

Search for the Mad Hatter

BEFORE THE SUN had even begun to crest the horizon, Alice slipped through the mirror to Wonderland. She changed her library shift at the last minute to give her the weekend, but hoped that Heather would assume she was there and not come looking for her. Adrianna knew full well where she was, but Heather was getting much more involved with her life than she was comfortable with right now. She had plenty of other things to worry about.

Despite how many things she needed to do there, none of her trips to Wonderland lately had been productive. The Hatter was still missing, the Queen was still moving, and she still had no idea where Matt was or how to return the hearts to the people of Neverland. So far, she had determined that madness was a thing that helped to connect Wonderland to their hearts, and that Neverland needed to use a different signifier to make it work, but she did not know enough about them to figure out what that was.

Adam was waiting for her in the house today. "No news," he told her as soon as she came though the mirror. "The Jabberwocky tolerates us, but he won't listen."

"You need Adrianna," Alice said. "He loved her. He'd probably do whatever she told him to."

"You are not bringing Addie over here," he said. "There have been way too many close calls lately. The Queen of Hearts has just about cleared out Wonderland of anyone that still has a heart that isn't directly under the White King's protection or is from Neverland. It's getting bloody out there, Alice."

"Not that bloody," Alice said. "Removing hearts doesn't make anyone bleed."

Adam shook his head, looking more annoyed than anything else. "Seriously, I don't know how much more of this I can handle."

"You could go back," Alice said. "I can take you back over and look for Matt myself and then get him over there too."

"That's what you always say," Adam said.

He walked in silence next to Alice on the path. Alice jumped forward several steps as they moved, taking a few normal paces between each jump. Adam broke out into a run to keep up to her and Alice felt much more at home.

Her mind started to wander and she made a note — not for the first time — to make a list of everything she needed to do before the Bandersnatch took her away. She would help Adam finish whatever it was he was after and she would bring him back. And she would find the Mad Hatter. And then she would find Matt. And she would find someone who could return the hearts and teach them how. And then she would be done.

Alice stopped in the middle of the path and looked up. "You know what I haven't tried yet?" she asked, realizing that she'd been very silly this whole time. "His coat. He would probably still have that. We keep finding top hats all over the place, but he's probably only got one coat."

"You tried his shoes that once," Adam pointed out. "And you couldn't remember what they looked like and you found a talking bird."

"That was an honest mistake," Alice said, waving him off. "It could have happened to anyone. And lots of people have the same shoes. That wasn't my fault."

"Maybe you should take a break," he said. "You've seemed kind of stressed lately. And when people get stressed around here, they start to go a little crazy."

Alice stiffened at the accusation and looked around for something else she could try. "I think I remember what the coat looks like," she insisted. "Bright and patchy, right?"

"*Sit*," Adam told her, putting a hand on her shoulder and forcing her to the path. They slipped around to the back of the tree so they could at least stay out of sight and Adam sat her down, trying to keep her from moving around too much or trying to go off and tracking down the Mad Hatter without him.

"Tiger Lily's noticed too," he said. "She thinks Wonderland is getting to you in a bad way. Or maybe those books are. You're a bit off lately. And you keep insisting that I just go back every time you come."

"That's because you need to go back," Alice told him. "You said it yourself. It's dangerous here. And you don't belong here."

"Neither do you."

"Actually, I do," Alice said. "I was six when I came here the first time and it hasn't let me stop coming back since school started. You can actually leave if you just let me take you back over before you get stuck here forever. And I really need you and Matt to go back."

"But you're here," Adam said. "And the Cheshire Cat can go back and forth too."

"If you think he's going to take you back—"

"I don't, but I know you will when everything's done," Adam told her. "I mean, sure I'm missing a couple years of school, but I can make that up no problem later. I'm actually doing something important here. I don't see why I need to leave until I see it out."

Alice shook her head and let out a frustrated noise. "Because I'm not going to be able to take you back forever," she told him. "I didn't want you to worry. I know you're happy here, but you don't belong here. You need to go back. I don't care if everyone over there isn't even going to notice that you're gone forever. You need to go back before it's too late."

"What? What do you mean before it's too late? Are you going to lose this ability to go through the mirrors?"

Alice kept shaking her head, feeling the stress of it starting to spill over. She very carefully kept her tears in check, remembering the river that came out of it the last time. "I made a bet with the Bandersnatch," she told him. "If I can't send him away before the end of this school year, he's going to take me and I'll be gone forever. I won't be able to get you back out anymore. You're going to be stuck in here. You and Matt, wherever he is. I still need to find him too."

"You talked about this before, didn't you?" he asked, eyes narrowing as he tried to remember. "I thought you were kidding. There can't really be a thing out there coming for you. Not outside of here."

"He's called the Bandersnatch," Alice told him. "Do you remember when you were trying to look up Evan even though he's your brother and you didn't know why you had all these files like you were trying to figure out who he was? And the emails? That was the Bandersnatch. He got traded to the Bandersnatch and when someone gets traded to him, you forget that they ever existed at all. And I made a bet that I could get rid of the Bandersnatch and if I did, he'd let everyone else he had in his garden go. But if I can't, I go into the garden."

"How is something like that even out there?"

"It came out of the same book as the Jabberwocky," Alice said.

"But you still have that book," Adam said. "Isn't there something in there about how to deal with it? You have all those things about how to make the Jabberwocky come and calling things in there so there must be something."

"There might be," Alice admitted, remembering the fire notes. If the flame worked on that book as well, there might have been something in the margins that would help her figure it out, but it was too late now. "But I traded the book to him."

"You *what*? Why?"

Alice shook her head, bringing her knees up to her chest. "The deal was until I finished middle school," Alice said. "I needed to get back the month that Tiger Lily had me trapped or else my parents wouldn't let me go back. I had to."

They sat in a long moment of silence. Alice didn't know what else to say. She wasn't prepared to tell him any of that today, but it came out anyway and she was unprepared for anything that came of it. She hadn't realized how much it was weighing on her and telling him was only making her more nervous. She wished he was Adrianna instead and they were in a place where her tears weren't going to flood the area and wash them far away. She took a deep breath and made herself calm down.

"I need to get you and Matt out of here before that happens," Alice told him. "You can stay until it's almost the end of the year, but once that happens, I won't have any time left. It's my fault you're both stuck in here, so I need to at least fix that."

"There has to be another way," Adam said. "You can't just—"

"It won't be so bad," she said. "No one will even remember I was ever there. No one will have to miss me or be sad about it."

"There has to be—"

"It's fine," Alice told him firmly. She didn't want to talk about it anymore. It was hard enough to hold in the tears and she was feeling very heavy and sore from trying to keep them in. She needed a distraction and something else to think about. "We have to find the Mad Hatter, right?"

"We don't have to today," Adam insisted. "We can wait and…"

Alice didn't hear the rest of what he proposed, her hand catching on the fabric of what felt like the Mad Hatter's coat. She had the image of it in her mind and she let herself be pulled along, getting up to follow it as it moved through the fog. She had been here before, the swampy lands mashing under her feet and making her regretting her choice of running shoes.

The Mad Hatter was in front of her with a top hat still on his head. They had already picked up seven, but it seemed this one was no smaller than usual. She opted not to think about it, her eyes instead trailing down his coat to eye level where there was a hand sized hole in his back leading to where his heart should be.

She looked around her and found that they were not alone. He moved slowly through the swamp and led several others at a glacial pace as they tried to get over and through the muck.

Alice took a better look at everyone around her, finding most of them dressed for battle, no matter how small an anthropomorphic woodland creature or unsuited for it they actually were. There were a lot of bears in this party accompanying the squirrels and mice, all wearing various finery and carrying weapons that she doubted they knew how to use.

Alice looked at the Hatter and tried to remain calm

despite her heart hammering in her chest. "Pardon me," she said, being as polite as she could manage while wading slowly through the muck with everyone else. She tugged lightly on his sleeve to get his attention. "Might I ask where you and your band are headed through such a terrible path?"

"We are on a mission for our Queen," the Hatter said, none of his madness leaking through as he spoke. The fact that he wasn't chiding her for rudely interrupting his walk was unsettling enough. The lack of any of the madness under his words chilling to her.

"And what mission might that be?" Alice asked. She kept her voice calm and curious.

"We are to go to the new land and take it for our Queen," he said. He stopped the march and everyone else around him did the same, settling in formation. He turned to face Alice, back straight and peering down his nose at her. "If anyone should oppose us, we are to remove their heads and bring their hearts back to our Queen."

"That doesn't sound very nice," Alice said. She was getting the sense from the sight of the sword at the Mad Hatter's side that she might actually be in very real trouble right now. "Couldn't you just talk? Maybe have a nice tea party instead?"

The Hatter's hand went to his sword, not drawing it but gripping the handle. The rest of his party followed him and Alice backed away from them, stumbling in the swamp and barely managing to keep her footing. "Do you seek to oppose us?" the Hatter asked.

"No!" Alice said, perhaps a little more insistent and panicked than she intended. "Of course not. I would never seek to oppose a Queen. That would be silly, don't you agree?"

The Mad Hatter loosened his grip on the sword handle. Alice relaxed, her mind spinning as she tried to come up with some way to stall them or to make it all take much longer than they intended to get to their destination.

"You are going the long way, though," she said. "To get to the other world, I mean. There's a much shorter way."

"A straight line is the shortest path."

Alice blinked at him for a moment before she managed to readjust herself. There was no madness here, which meant that she probably shouldn't rely on Wonderland logic to get her out of this. Instead, she could rely on the normal stuff that she used on the doctors and everyone else instead.

"But you're going through the swamp," she said. "The mud is slowing you down much more than if you were to take a slight detour and walk along the solid ground. You must have noticed that your progress has been much slower than expected since you entered the swamp."

The Mad Hatter continued to relax his grip on the blade. He made a nod, considering what she had to say as if it were perfectly logical and it wasn't spoken out of turn or said in any manner he could consider rude. Alice reminded herself that this was what she'd asked for on more than one occasion, no matter how disturbing it was to see now. She could handle letting her wish be fulfilled this once and never wish it again.

"The swamp is going to slow you down because of how marshy it is and how difficult it is to walk through. There's also a lake up ahead, which you would have to swim through if you wanted to get to the other side and swimming with that much metal is probably going to be difficult. That's not mentioning the forest and whatever you might run into there that might slow you down as well."

"You have a fair point," the not so Mad Hatter said.

"I can help you find several good routes if you need a hand. Or," she said, an idea striking her that might make it last a little longer, "There's a person I know who can help you navigate the way through to the other world. He's quite good."

"We will not be taking the routes suggested by anyone from Wonderland," The Mad Hatter said, once more growing aggressive. He didn't have his hand on his sword any longer, but he stood square to face her and Alice could feel the menace coming off of him. "We will find our own path that will surely be faster than anything they could suggest for us."

"Oh, he's not from Wonderland," Alice told him. "He's from another world entirely. One of those ones that the Queen of Hearts would very much like to have for herself. He'll know the best way to get back home for himself. He actually is from a different one than the one you're heading to. If you really want, you could probably ask him to find out how to get to his world as well. The Queen might be pleased if you came back having brought her two worlds instead of one."

The Mad Hatter considered this, his eyes glazing over as he did so, until they cleared again and looked down at her. "We will do only as our Queen commands," he said. "This guide will lead us only to the world beyond Wonderland. We care not for the world he is from."

Alice smiled, hoping that she could actually pull this off. "Excellent," she said. "You are going to need to just head out of the swamp and he will meet with you on the edge. It's just out that way. Keep going until you find a small house in the woods that is filled with several sleeping people and he will be in there. He collects them from the forest, the ones that your Queen had determined are not good enough for her army."

"The ones who will not forfeit their hearts," The Mad Hatter said, a sharp edge to his voice.

"Yes, those," Alice said awkwardly. "He's just cleaning up the forest so that the Queen doesn't have to deal with them any longer. He'll help you find the edge of Wonderland and take you right over. It should only be a day or two to get out of the swamp. Once you do, walk along the edge until you find a path lined with cottonwood. It will lead you right to the house."

"You will lead us to him," the Mad Hatter said.

"I'm afraid I have another engagement," Alice said, dancing back in the muck as best she could and curtsying as low as she had to without getting too dirty. "I will tell him you are coming and to watch for you. It will give him the time to plan the best route for you."

"Tell him if he tries to double-cross us, we will remove his head."

Alice took a steadying breath and nodded. "Of course. His heart will belong to the Queen. It already does," she insisted. "Farewell. And best of luck."

Alice stepped away into the swamp and behind a tree, reappearing back around the tree where she had left Adam behind. She may have made a very bad mistake, but it was too late to turn back now.

Adam wasn't there and she tried to think. This was bad enough, but she needed to stall the Mad Hatter. Adam would be able to lead them in a winding route around Wonderland. If he could just lead them into enough traps to slow them down, it might give them enough time to try and sort out what to do.

And what they needed was the Mad Hatter's heart.

Shaking her head, she had an idea, though it was likely a

bad one. She thought of the headband Tiger Lily often wore and reached out for it. She appeared behind her a moment later, though she was there for only a fraction of a second. As soon as Tiger Lily felt the touch, she turned and grabbed Alice by the arm. She spun Alice around and pinned her to the ground, blade at her throat.

"Alice of Wonderland," she said in recognition, stepping back and offering Alice a hand up. "You are not one who should sneak up on people. You are becoming far too much like that cat. It is treacherous behaviour."

"I need you to do something," Alice said, taking Tiger Lily by the hand and looking around to see where they were. They were on a cliff edge, the familiar growling of the Jabberwocky emanating from behind them. She knew where this was, feeling the edge of Wonderland just where she knew it would be and feeling the pulsing edge starting to encroach on the edge of her mind. She could feel the madness seeping in and tried to keep herself together, but she would only have a moment here.

"I need you to find the Mad Hatter's heart and bring it to me," Alice said.

"You expect me to find it," she said, a statement rather than a question.

"You're a tracker. Track it. I need to go."

Alice stepped away, dropping off the edge of the cliff and

landing back down in the forest. She needed to find Adam and think about the ramifications of what she'd actually done later. There had to be something she could use to find him. He had always come to her at this point and she didn't pay attention to the things he was wearing or the common things he always had on him. She knew he carried mushrooms to change his size so he could ride on the local wildlife when he needed to get somewhere, but other than that there was nothing she had to go on.

She went through the forest and started to try and put together what she had just done. There was a plan there, she was sure, but she needed to figure out just what it was. She could feel herself starting to shake and forced herself to keep breathing, pinching the inside of her wrist to assure herself that she wasn't dreaming. She had to pull it together. She needed to figure out what she was doing.

The Mad Hatter. She had found the Mad Hatter. She was sending the Mad Hatter this way. It would take them about a day to get through the swamp and head over this way. She knew she had done that much. Adam would take over after that point. He would find some way to keep the Mad Hatter from getting to the end point until Alice managed to figure out a way to get his heart back into him. Tiger Lily would find his heart and he would be returned to normal. And whatever his plan was for the Queen of Hearts could happen. And hopefully Adam would come home after that.

If he survived leading the Mad Hatter around. There was always the possibility that he would not be fast enough after he angered the Mad Hatter and his head would be removed. He would just have to not say anything stupid for a little while and not get anyone mad at him. He could do that much. He had to.

Alice took a deep breath and she felt like she might cry. She forced herself calm, not wanting to drown anyone and not wanting to draw more attention to herself than she needed to. She just needed to tell Adam. She would warn him that there was a Mad Hatter coming for him and there was a plan in place.

Down the path, she saw something coming closer to her and she moved to the side, stepping behind a tree and staying very quiet. It couldn't be the Mad Hatter already. She didn't know what she would do if it was the Mad Hatter already. There was too much that she would need to do and not enough time to do it in if he'd somehow found a quick way out of the swamp.

"For once, I am not late," the white figure said as he came down the forest lane. Alice peered around the tree, finding it was a well-dressed White Rabbit, looking calm and relaxed as he pocketed his pocket watch. "For once. For only this once, though I assume that this once will already be one time too many. But once is still better than never, so I shall revel in the once."

Alice found herself checking his chest for the hole that should surely be there. Instead, she found that he had his heart back. She could hardly remember but she did return his heart at some point. She must have. She had no idea when, but it must have happened because here he was, looking more content and not panicked for once in his life as he hopped down the path.

Alice let herself slip back out, looking curiously at the White Rabbit and he stopped in the road to greet her. He was in bright spirits and looked back in a kind greeting. "Hello!" he said. "A wonderful day to not be late, isn't it?" he asked.

"As wonderful day as every other day," Alice said. She felt surly, almost wanting someone to tell her again that she was rude. Something to make up for the Hatter not doing it. "The weather here only falters when I do. And I have been so careful not to falter. You should thank me."

The White Rabbit smiled. "Alice," he said, hopping closer and putting an arm around her shoulders, leading her down the path. "Why, I almost think you were asking me to tell you how horrid your manners were. I would imagine you are doing it on purpose! But surely that cannot be the case."

"So no one around here thinks I'm rude anymore," Alice said. "This place really has gone mad."

The White Rabbit laughed at her. "It is too good of a day to be allowed to be bothered by something so trivial as manners."

Alice stepped away from him, looking at him carefully and looking very closely to make sure his heart was still there. The White Rabbit smiled and continued past Alice, expecting her to fall in step behind him. Alice made sure there was enough there to be sure there was no hole behind him before she walked behind him.

"Do you know where Adam is?"

"Have you tried looking for him in the place he currently is?" the White Rabbit asked.

Alice looked back at him and was certain that this was the only thing that would be an acceptable answer from someone who still had their heart. "I would if I knew where that was," Alice said.

"Well you should try to find that," the White Rabbit said. "Perhaps you could ask him and find out where he is that way."

"Perhaps," she agreed. "Are you heading home?"

"Home is always the place I try to head," the White Rabbit said. "It is, however, far more elusive than I remember. It has been so long that I've been gone that I wonder if my home will still remember me as fondly as I remember it. If I remember, you have seen my house before. Perhaps it would remember you more fondly."

Alice looked at him with a straight face. She remembered growing so large in that house that she broke it. She wasn't about to think that his house would think any more kindly of her after that. "You should know that your house has been in use since you've been gone," Alice said.

"I do hope it's being used for its intended purpose," the White Rabbit said. "I am afraid a house doesn't work so well as a bowling ball or a rolling pin."

"It is being used to house people," Alice told him, choosing her words carefully.

"I should hope so," the White Rabbit said. "A house is not really a house if it is not housing someone."

"These people are heartless."

"That's not terribly nice to say," the White Rabbit said. "I am sure they are perfectly nice people. It is not polite to judge someone so quickly, Alice."

Alice shook her head feeling the frustration swelling up in her again. "No, they don't have their hearts."

"They may still be perfectly respectable people."

Alice shook her head. "I'm sorry. I don't have time for this. I need to find Adam." She had to warn him of what was going to happen and she had to do a lot of things before she went back to school. There was almost too much, but she was going to do it. She just needed to finish this, get Adam out, and then she could get Matt. And then she could be done at last.

"You look tired, Alice," the White Rabbit said. Alice wasn't sure why, but he sounded a lot closer than he had a moment ago.

She felt something club her hard across the back of the head and Alice wasn't able to feel anything else after that.

CHAPTER 12

The Plan

ALICE AWOKE ON the couch of the White Rabbit's house, surrounded by several other sleeping figures. She was laid out on a couch that had been spared of bodies for now, though she wasn't sure how long she had been lying there. She checked her watch to check the time.

Three in the morning. Monday. She was in so much trouble.

Alice scrambled off the couch, already feeling dizzy from getting up too fast, and she fell on the floor. She started to try to get to her feet when a fan poked at her throat, keeping her still and pushing her back down to the ground.

"Not yet," came a gentle voice of the White Rabbit. "It would be very rude of you to leave before I served you breakfast and you wouldn't want to leave before thanking your host, would you?"

Alice stayed down, not sure what it was he was looking for. He kept the fan there in threat, though nothing else
about him seemed remotely threatening. She wasn't sure
what she was supposed to do and waited at the bottom of the
fan.

But she needed to get home. She had been gone too long.
When he started to move the fan, Alice got to her feet and
stood in front of the mirror. She had to go.

"No you don't," Adam said, pulling her back before she
could go through. "You aren't going anywhere until you tell
me what's going on."

Alice spun around to meet him, looking down at her
watch and trying desperately to pull free of his grip. "I need
to go."

"The White Rabbit said you were looking for me," he
said. "What's going on? What happened?"

Alice shook her head. Right. She had to do that. She
relaxed in his grip and took a breath, trying to get her head
back together and get an idea of what was going to happen
from here on out. She could do this.

"The Mad Hatter is coming this way," she said. "He might
already almost be here. He was about a day out in the swamp."

"What?"

"I found him," Alice said. "I told him that it was going to
take too long to go the way he was going and told him to come

this way. I told him that there would be someone who could lead him to the other world they were heading for. I said it was you," Alice said. There was a stabbing pain in the back of her head. She felt very light headed all of a sudden. She moved away from the mirror, around the people on the ground. "You seemed like the sort he would want to talk to, after all. You are very interested in wandering around aimlessly, so you should be perfect to make them go around aimlessly. Don't tell them that, though. Or perhaps do. It's quite rude to not mention your intentions, unless those intentions are rude themselves. And I suppose these are quite rude intentions."

"Rabbit..." Adam said, watching her.

"They might ask you how to get back home, but you wouldn't show them if you did know. You don't even want to go back yourself, even if it means getting stuck here. But that's alright, because you know where everything is. Give them a grand tour of Wonderland and keep them away from Never-land. That's what the other world is, you know. Where Tiger Lily is from. They have zombies and it's not terribly nice. You shouldn't let them go there. While you do that, Tiger Lily is going to try and find the Mad Hatter's heart and when she does, BAM!"

Alice popped back up in front of Adam, legs hooked on the ceiling beams and swinging down to look at him. He backed away at the sudden appearance of her. "That's when I can put his heart back in him and then you can get the Jabberwocky back. And then you'll be able to do whatever it is you need to do. And then I can stop worrying about you at last."

"Alice, what are you talking about?"

"I don't know that he'll really *need* to get much further than staying right in here," the White Rabbit told her. "You don't know much about my house, though you have let yourselves live here for long enough."

"This all sounds insane," Adam said. "So, wait, you want *Tiger Lily* to find the Mad Hatter's heart?"

"Of course," Alice said, still swinging from the ceiling. She let herself drop and landed softly on the couch. "You're going to be busy of course. And she's a tracker. She should be able to track down his heart. I'm sure it will all work out just fine if you can distract the Mad Hatter for long enough."

"Alice, Tiger Lily can't find the hearts," Adam said. "She can't use the binoculars. They just won't work for her."

"What binoculars?"

Adam pulled out a pair of opera glasses from his back pocket, the handle looking far too short to be intact. She was almost certain that they had been broken at some point, but they were very intricate looking nonetheless. He held them up as if she should know what they were, but Alice couldn't tell for the life of her what she was supposed to get out of them.

"I got them from an old witch on the edge of Wonderland," he said. "They let me see where the Queen of Hearts keeps most of— No, this is stupid. We're trashing this idea."

"I do believe I know where the Queen of Hearts would have kept the Mad Hatter's heart," the White Rabbit said, cocking his head to one side and trying to read Alice's expression. "I daresay she keeps some hearts in that dreadful room of hers like trophies, but there are others that she simply cannot fit there. Some hearts don't play well with others, you see. And some she needs to keep much more careful watch over. She needs her generals to be where they will play nicely and she will be sure to make sure they will continue to do so. She keeps those ones in her throne instead of that room."

"I can get that," Alice said. "I think I could get the whole throne here right now. That's easy."

Adam stopped her before she could do anything. "You need to not do anything else today," Adam told her. "You're losing it, Alice. You need to go back."

"He's right," the White Rabbit said. He smiled gently at her and nodded back to her wrist. "A girl should do well to be sure never to be late or she will be forever rushing to her next appointment. And I know what it's like to be quite late all of the time."

"You are far too normal to be here," Adam said.

The White Rabbit smiled conspiratorially. "There are a few of us here who are like that," he said. He didn't elaborate, but Alice didn't want him to. Whatever that conversation was happening over there, it wasn't nearly as interesting as what was going on outside. There were people coming down the path, looking all covered in muck and like they'd had a very bad time of getting out of the swamp. At the front, a man in a top hat kept his face neutral, but his hand on his sword as he brought them to a halt a short ways away. They remained just out of sight of the path and at the very furthest distance down the path so that they could still see the house, but they were not anywhere near entering it.

"I think they're here," Alice said.

"Already?" the White Rabbit asked, moving around his house, carefully hopping over the bodies that were strewn around. "Oh, I do hope none of you put one of these in my bed."

"I'll go out," Adam said, taking a deep breath.

"Be careful not to make him mad," Alice told him. "He seems like he wants to cut off a head."

"I should be okay," Adam said with a wink as he got outside.

"Just keep them out there for a few minutes," the White Rabbit said. "I think I should be able to give you a hand once that's done."

"Do you need me to do anything?" Alice asked.

"Oh, no," the White Rabbit said. "We should be fine.

When you come back, we should have a heart for you to put back."

"What are you going to do?"

The White Rabbit smiled. "If you'd like, you can watch." He collected a watering can from his windowsill and went outside to fill it with water from the well.

Alice got to her feet and sat back down onto a branch of one of the trees outside of the White Rabbit's house where she would be able to watch everything happen. She kept herself hidden among the leaves and stayed very quiet, though she was ready to interfere if anything happened.

"Hello," Adam said, smiling and bowing to the Mad Hatter. "I was told you needed a hand getting back to the other world."

"So the girl did come back here," the Mad Hatter said, looking at Adam crookedly. "I think I knew her once. I think I knew you once."

Alice could tell just how unsettled Adam was at seeing and talking to the Mad Hatter like this. This wasn't natural, she knew, but Adam certainly looked like he handled it better than she did. He put on that sleazy salesman smile, just a little charm with the promise of a bite if anyone got too friendly. It was apparently what Heather had liked so much about him.

"I'm sure I would remember if I met someone such as

yourself before," he said. "And I don't believe we've met. Please, call me Mark. And you are?"

"Hatter," he said shortly. "You will show me and my men to the other world. We must take it for our Queen. Any disobedience on your part will result in the removal of your head. You will pledge your heart to our Queen."

"Of course, of course," Adam said smoothly. "But first, I need to collect the rest of my supplies. As I'm sure Alice mentioned, I'm not from around here. I need a few things to keep me going that you aren't going to need so much of, so you'll pardon me if I need just a moment to ready them before we head out. It will only be a moment. Come, you can rest and clean off in the house."

Hatter went along, as did the rest of his party, following Adam towards the house. Alice went closer, but she ran out of trees to hide in. Reluctantly, she went back into the house to watch as the White Rabbit came in to join her. He settled in next to her at the window, looking through a different crack in the curtain with a very different sort of madness in his eye. Gently, he eased the window soundlessly open so they could hear. He smiled, watching the strange flowers that he grew that were made entirely of hands.

Adam walked them through the garden, telling them of the path as the Hatter asked for more information, outlining what was actually a very accurate path to get to Neverland.

Alice was impressed, but worried. That wasn't how the plan was supposed to go. He was supposed to stall them instead of leading them right there.

And then Alice saw why. Behind him as he led them through the garden and toward the house, she found there was something else moving. The flowers grew hands instead of leaves. There were claws that grew out of the ground. They reached out and snapped around the ankles of those in the back and to the sides. They made no noise as they were caught. Their metal attire jangled as they tried to pull free.

"We'll have to find some way around the people who have settled on the plains," Adam said, not paying any attention as they fell victim to the garden behind him, keeping the Hatter's flickering attention. "Best not to get too tired fighting them, really. There's much worse that you'll have to worry about on the other side of Wonderland's wall. They're trapped in a lot of night and have a lot of their dead coming back to life. They never stop wandering and don't usually die when they are killed."

"You seem to know a lot about what exists over there."

"Before you'll make it to the other side, though, you're going to have to get past the Jabberwocky. But I don't think you'll have a problem with him."

"Why not?"

"Because you won't be seeing him for a bit."

Adam turned back as the plants caught the Mad Hatter, smiling as he looked on the garden. The hands were pulling most of his men down below the ground already and most of them were buried to the waist in plants that had already snatched away their weapons. The plants continued to thrive around them and their leaves grabbed them and continued to pull them down.

The Hatter went to his waist and drew his sword. "Off with your head!" he cried, swinging at Adam.

Alice jumped at the movement, but she had nothing to worry about. Adam pulled out a tomahawk from the back of his shirt and blocked the sword, getting in close enough to grab the Hatter's sword hand. He twisted until the Hatter let go of the sword and smacked him hard in the face with the axe.

Hatter went down, taken quickly by the hands, and Adam bent down to swipe the hat off of his head. He brought the hat inside and smiled at Alice, putting it on her head.

"Here," Adam said. "We'll get word to you somehow when we figure out where the Mad Hatter's heart is."

"How did you do that?" Alice asked, looking at the White Rabbit.

The White Rabbit ushered her away from the window. "I used to be quite good at tag," he said with a wink.

Alice accepted this without much argument and walked

back through the mirror and back into her room. At this time in the morning, she was content to just crawl into bed and get a little sleep until the morning. She could deal with the fact that she'd gone missing for the weekend without expecting it again. She would be fine. Just a few more things left to do before she disappeared.

She put the Hatter's hat into the hiding place with the books and stripped out of her muddy clothing before heading to sleep.

CHAPTER 13

Another Break In

WHEN MORNING CAME far too early, she noticed her side of the room seemed to be out of sorts. Someone had gone through the suitcase at the bottom of her wardrobe again, as well as through the books in her drawers. Her computer was untouched, but there were little things of hers that had gotten put just a little out of place. She knew there was someone who had been through it and she was pretty sure she knew who. And she was not going to deal with it right now.

Peter lingered just on the outside of her vision whenever she looked up, but she refused to let herself pay him any attention. She didn't need that right now. She could do without the extra stress. She needed to focus on getting more than a few things done.

She spent the next couple days isolating herself in her room when she wasn't in class. Though she said it was because she didn't feel well, her attention was on the red book. There were too many people who needed her to know how to work that book, from putting the hearts back in Wonderland folk to Neverland folk. Adam might come back willingly when Wonderland was returned to normal, which meant she would need to come up with a more efficient way to do that.

Not to mention she needed to figure out how to make it work for Neverland. She wasn't sure what it was that separated the two, but she looked more closely through the words she chose to make it work and found that she was tying the heart to the madness and the person whose madness it belonged to. Neverland people did not have the same madness requirement. They were not mad in quite the same way and therefore she wouldn't be able to measure and find them in the same way.

Which left her trying to figure out what else she could use as a signifier. There were so many pages in this book with so much information in it that she relied on her notes more than anything. The notes outlined things that she wouldn't be able to think of on her own. They were about how every-thing worked and they were the dictionary of terms and the structure. They removed the theory and kept all the practical elements for her to actually work with.

There was something in here that she wasn't seeing. She knew there was something small that was missing. She just didn't know what she could use instead of madness in that one component of the spell that would make the hearts go back and it drove her nuts. There had to be something else. And there was unfortunately only one person here who might be able to tell her what that was.

Peter appeared of his own accord at Alice's window. She didn't know how he kept managing to open the window on his own when she was so careful to lock it, but he did. He watched her from a distance, but she knew he was there and she needed the break from staring at the book for now.

"What is it, Peter?" she asked, closing the book and computer. She debated if she wanted to actually turn around, or rest her head on the desk for a moment first.

"Kevin's getting worried about you," he said. "He said you've done this before. And Heather thinks there's someone coming after you that you aren't talking about."

"Then maybe you should stop breaking in here and trying to find the books," Alice said, picking the book up and slipping it back into the ceiling. "Seriously, I think you've hit everywhere I used to hide them. Where else do you have to check?"

"I'm not looking!" he insisted. "Really! I don't want to touch those things. I don't know how you do it."

"I will *give* you one of them if it will make you leave me alone."

"There's someone else who's doing it," he said.

"Why are you here, Peter?" Alice asked again.

Peter looked around and Alice turned to look at him, seeing that he looked nervous. "Can we talk not here?" he asked. "I know I'm not supposed to be in your room because you're a girl and all, so maybe outside?"

Alice rolled her eyes and locked the door, grabbing her key before she appeared outside the building. Peter landed next to her, walking along with her in the waning daylight. There was still enough light out that dinner would still be served and Alice realized she hadn't eaten yet. She headed to the cafeteria with Peter, not paying any attention to how hesitant he was about them staying so close to people. He may have wanted solitude, but she needed a snack.

"Have you gone back to Neverland?" he asked. They had gotten food by the time it finally came out of his mouth. "You were gone all weekend. I saw that you weren't really there. You went to Wonderland, right?"

Alice lead them to a quiet table near the window and away from the rest of the eyes around them. She nodded at Peter's question, feeling very tired.

"I'm not visiting Neverland when I'm over there," Alice said. "Neverland isn't my responsibility. It's yours. I'm just trying to make sure everything is okay in Wonderland right now. And right now, unfortunately, there's some of Wonderland that's trying to get across the border and slip into Neverland."

"Why would they want to do that?" Peter asked. He looked horrified.

"Because the Queen of Hearts wants it," Alice said. "She thinks that it will be like Wonderland. But I already know what happens when you try to remove the hearts out of someone from Neverland and it doesn't really work out so well."

"What happens?"

"Nothing."

"That's not that bad."

"Not that kind of nothing," Alice said. She picked up a spoon off her tray and put it between them, giving Peter a view of inside the White Rabbit's house. He balked at the people inside, probably recognizing one or two of the faces as they curled up around their hearts. They clutched them and kept them close, looking desperately at them as if they couldn't remember why it was important or what to do with them, but that it was still the most important thing in the world to them.

"I've been trying to figure out how to put them back," Alice told him, taking the spoon back and using it on her pudding. "I almost had it, I thought, but I can't figure out what else I need to link it to. In Wonderland, everyone is mad, but it's in a bit of a different way. That's what keeps everyone going. They're all mad there. But in Neverland, I don't know anything about the place except for the zombies, so I have no idea what I'm supposed to do with it. How does it work there?"

Peter's eyes stayed on the table where the spoon had been. He shook his head. "I don't know," he said. "I don't know how anything *worked* there. It just *did*."

"There has to be something," Alice mused. "In Wonderland, if something happened, it's because some mad logic made it happen. When things happen in Neverland, something must make it happen."

He shrugged. "You just think it and it happens," he said. "You want food and food is there. You want adventure and adventure is there. You want anything and it's there if it's not people. You had to get people yourself. You…"

Peter fell quiet, another thought occurring to him. The colour seeped away from his face.

Alice nodded into her pudding. "I think I can use that," she said, thinking back to her notes. Her eyes scanned the cafeteria to make sure no one was paying attention to her. She reached to one side of her and found the laptop still sitting on her desk. She unplugged it and pulled it out of her room to the cafeteria. She put it in front of her and started to muddle through her notes.

She searched for imagination and dreams, for whimsy and fun and play, and eventually found enough notes that she thought she could use. "I think I might have figured it out," she said, highlighting what might be relevant. She would have to get some paper to work out some of the finer details, but there was enough here that she could put together something rough that might work for the people of Neverland.

When she looked up, Peter was there looking over her shoulder. "That stuff looks complicated," he said. "Why can't it just be easy? Like flying."

Alice shut the laptop and put it under the table, placing it back on her desk in her room and pulling her hands back empty. "Because then anyone could do it," Alice told him, getting up from the seat and starting to walk towards the door. Peter followed in step behind her. "You really just wanted an update on Neverland, though? Because you could go there and see for yourself. I still don't know how you managed to get out of there in the first place."

Peter pointed up at the sky. "Just go to the second star on the right and straight on until morning," he said. "It's not hard."

"If you can fly," Alice said.

"All you need is some fairy dust and some happy thoughts," Peter said. "It's not hard."

"So go back and see for yourself what's going on in Neverland," Alice said. "It looked like it could use some saving. Maybe you could actually save it."

Peter crossed his arms over his head as he walked. "I've saved it so many times already," he said. "It's time someone else did it."

"Because you're scared of the zombies."

"I'm not scared of anything!"

"Except zombies."

"Those books *are* turning you evil."

Alice let out a laugh, but more of a determined one than anything else. If she could get this done, then she might be able to give the White Rabbit and Adam a little backup while she waited for them to get the hearts back from the Queen of Hearts. She just needed to get back into the dorms and get her hands on some paper so that she could go back to working on it again.

"I can try to help the people from Neverland in Wonderland," Alice told him. "That's all I'm going to do. You're going to have to find someone else to save the place for you."

Peter shook his head. "Someone else will do it. I don't need you to do it."

"Really?" Alice asked, not believing him at all.

"I just need you to tell me when someone stepped up and saved it," Peter told her. "John will do it. He just needs to suck it up and then he'll do it."

"Just keep your people from coming to Wonderland," Alice said. "It's not really working out that well for them."

"You just need to stop luring them over there!" Peter said. "You have stuff like trees with fridges in them. That's not fair."

Alice would argue that the fact that Neverland didn't have fridges growing on trees was a point in his favour, but she opted not to argue the point for now. He would either go back and help save Neverland or not and she wasn't going to make him go one way or the other on the matter. At the moment, he looked like he was content to never go back at all, settling in well with school for the time being and, besides his attempts to find the books in her room, he was doing just fine at being a student.

She saw Joe and Travis walking towards the cafeteria and offered them a brief wave, but they seemed too distracted to pay her any attention. The sight of them reminded her that she should email Lori and see how she was doing with school. It was her senior year as well and, if the pair of them were any indication, she was likely just as stressed out and exhausted.

Yet another thing. She shook her head and smiled, turning back to Peter. Lori would come later, after she got all these notes down and figured out the right spell for Neverland. She'd waited this long already, so a few hours more shouldn't make a difference.

"You're a lot better at being a student than Cat was," Alice told him.

"It's kind of boring," Peter said. "I used to spend all day hanging out with mermaids and fighting pirates and making the Lost Boys do stuff for me. Now it's all sitting down and reading books."

"Some of it's interesting, though," Alice said.

"Maybe," Peter said. "There were all these big battles that we're reading about now and those sound like they would have been a lot of fun! But Tiger Lily would have never let any of these guys invade her and take her over. The Indians here should get her to teach them how to defend their lands so that they don't get tricked by stupid blankets."

Alice wasn't sure Peter quite knew that Neverland was a very different place from the real world, but she was content at least with the fact that he could not only read, but process the information enough to know that things were a bit messed up. "She wouldn't think they were coming in peace, anyway," Alice agreed. "Have you been telling a lot of people—"

"Alice!" Adrianna came running after her with Sarah and Robert in tow, looking frantic. "Where were you?"

"Sorry," Alice said. "Peter just needed a hand with something and I needed to get something to eat. I didn't mean to be gone for that long."

"Probably a good thing you were," Robert said. "How long were you gone for?"

Alice shrugged, looking to Peter. Peter was giving her a strange look like he couldn't figure out why she was lying and she decided that it would be best to keep him from talking for a little while. From the looks on everyone else's faces, she should be much more concerned than she was. "Not that long. Why? What's going on?"

"Someone broke in," Adrianna said. "The room was locked, but when I went in…"

Alice caught Adrianna in a hug, seeing that she needed it at the moment, though her mind was working. She glanced back at Peter, who gave her a look like she should have never doubted his innocence. She'd been with him the whole time, so that ruled him out. Had Cat gotten out of the mirror, then? Was it him going through her room while she wasn't looking, checking every place she had ever actually or thought about hiding the books in an attempt to find it?

"It's okay," Alice said. "We'll talk to Miss Amanda and change the locks."

"And maybe file a police report," Robert said.

Alice looked up at that, not sure what to make of it. She passed Adrianna off to Sarah for the moment and they all headed upstairs. "Adrianna, can you get Miss Amanda?" she asked.

Adrianna nodded and went down the hall while Alice went down to the other end where she was supposed to live.

Robert was behind her and Alice found the door locked, as Adrianna must have done after she saw what was in there. Alice unlocked the door and Robert stayed close behind her as she did so.

"You know," he said cautiously, looking around, "if you weren't gone for long, whoever did it might still be in there."

"I don't think someone's going to stick around after they get caught," Alice said, opening the door. "If they even thought Adrianna might have seen them, they probably left on their own."

Alice looked into the room from the doorway and she felt a wave of panic wash over her. Calm. She needed to stay calm.

It was just her side of the room again, but this time some-one had done some actual damage. Her covers were pulled aside and they had cut into her mattress right near where she used to hide the book. The pillows looked like they had also been slashed and her suitcase was thrown clear across the room, the bottom of her dresser looking like someone put a foot through it.

"That's not good," Alice said, looking around and step-ping into her room to get a better look. She went to the torn open suitcase, wondering what they were expecting to find in it this time that they hadn't found every time before. Her hand went under some clothing under the pretense of feeling around and she ran her fingers over the spine of both of the books as well as the Mad Hatter's hat, all safely hidden away in the ceiling.

"It looks like there's someone out to get you, Alice," Robert said, looking around. This time Alice couldn't think of a way to hide that fact, but she wasn't sure what she was supposed to do about any of this. Again, her computer full of notes from the books remained untouched. She knew just what they were after by the things that had been disturbed.

"I don't know why," Alice said, glancing over at the washroom. It had been left untouched this time, but she wasn't sure why everything had been destroyed this time to nearly this degree. Or at all. After Peter smashed the mirrors, all the searching in the room had done was move things a little out of the way. She didn't know someone would go through the trouble of cutting or smashing anything this time around.

"Who did you piss off?" Robert asked again, taking another look around and looking at the smashed bottom of her wardrobe. "Who knew you weren't here?"

Alice shrugged, closing the suitcase and leaving it in the middle of the floor. "Peter?" She glanced at the window and found it was open, though she was sure she'd closed and locked that as well when she left. She went back over and closed it again, trying to go through who else it might have been, but she came up with nothing. "I don't think I've gotten anyone mad lately."

"Lately," Robert said. "Think about it. Is there anyone from a while ago, maybe?"

Alice could run down a list of people who could have done it, but they should all be trapped on the other side of the mirror in Wonderland and Neverland. There shouldn't be anyone else unless there were more people out there like Peter who could fly, coming out of Neverland and looking to steal the books from her for Wendy or the Queen of Hearts. How they knew where she used to hide the books, though, was a mystery.

Miss Amanda came by a moment later, Robert moving out of the way. Miss Amanda ignored him, going to Alice's side instead and trying to keep her calm. She seemed to think there was a lot more troubling to Alice than it actually was. She brought Alice to her office to talk to her instead of letting her stay there in her room to make sure there was nothing actually missing.

"I'll need to call your parents about this," Miss Amanda said after she was sure Alice was okay and Alice told her that she had no idea who would do such a thing. "We need to tell them when these sorts of incidents happen."

Alice nodded. "Okay," she said as if Miss Amanda were asking her whether she wanted waffles or pancakes for breakfast. "They aren't going to want to do anything, though. They're busy."

"They'd still like to know."

Alice smiled in the way that was comfortable for her to do when adults didn't believe what she was saying. There was no point in arguing with Miss Amanda. She had already decided she knew what her parents were like and what Alice would need to be comforted by all this. There was a procedure there, probably, and Alice knew better than to fight it. It would only draw it out a lot longer.

"Is there anything going on at home?" Miss Amanda asked. "Is there a reason you think your parents are too busy to care that their daughter is having someone break into her room and tear it apart?"

"I think they're going to be filing for divorce," Alice told her. "You can ask them if they've started talking to each other again yet if you'd like. Ask Mom, because Dad will tell you nothing's wrong."

The look on Miss Amanda's face was worth telling her that. Alice didn't want to make a big deal out of this, but she didn't see anything wrong with making her feel as awkward about this conversation as Alice felt. She just wanted to get her computer, hole up somewhere with the red book and try to piece together how to return Neverland people their hearts. And then get back over there to see if she was right.

"If you ever feel the need to talk about any of this, my door is always open," she said finally. "For tonight, though,

I don't think it's a good idea for you to stay in your room for a while. I'm going to let you and Adrianna stay with Sarah and Heather for now until we can come up with an alternate arrangement."

"If you just replace the stuff that's broken, I'm okay with going back into the room," Alice said.

"We'll need to change the locks and check for security issues with the room before we let anyone back in there," Miss Amanda told her. "If both of you really want that room again, we can see what we can do. But for now, are you going to be okay staying with your friends?"

Alice nodded, though she wasn't happy about it. She wanted to do some more work and figure out everything else, but she wasn't going to be able to do that with Sarah and Heather around. Maybe she could figure it out once they were all asleep and retire to the library or somewhere that she could actually do some work.

Adrianna was waiting for her outside the door and swept her away the moment that she could, wanting to talk to her before Alice had the chance to slip off again. "Are you okay? Is the Cat back? Is it someone else?"

Alice smiled and shook her head, resisting the urge to laugh as she put both hands on Adrianna's shoulders. "I'm okay," Alice said. "This has been going on all semester.

They just haven't been breaking stuff since the time with the mirrors."

"All semester?" Adrianna asked. "Why didn't you tell me?"

Alice shrugged. "They never took anything," she said. "It was just some stuff moved a little. They're looking for the books. Everywhere that they've looked and broken and stuff has been places that I've hidden the books before. That part of my bed. The bottom of the dresser. In my desk. In the suitcase. They never tried to break anything before, though."

"Maybe they're getting mad," Adrianna said. "You hid them really well this time."

Alice nodded. "Probably a good thing, too. I don't want someone who's going to do that to get their hands on the books."

"Where did you hide them?" Adrianna asked. "I never see you put them away anymore. You just pull them out of nowhere."

"A place Matt told me about," Alice told her. "Kind of. Don't worry, no one can get to it except me. So, how much time is Sarah going to spend insisting on makeovers tonight?" Alice asked with a smile. "Because I'm betting we aren't going to get any sleep tonight."

Adrianna seemed content at that and they continued

moving. It wasn't long before Sarah and Heather were making them at home in their dorm, barricading the door just in case and doing their best to make their guests comfortable. They had school in the morning, though Alice and Adrianna were excused if they felt they needed it. Alice was ready to take them up on that offer, if only because it would give her a little time to work on the book. She needed to go back this weekend to help them out.

"I bet it was Nike," Heather said, crossing her arms and seeming to make a much grander statement than she was while Sarah rolled her eyes. "It had to be!" Heather insisted. "Who else could it possibly be?"

"He is a little unstable," Sarah said, Alice hearing more in her words than she said. She kept her eyes averted for now, but Alice could read that expression. Sarah likely remembered her time with the Bandersnatch, then her time being Nike's girlfriend to replace Alice after she rejected him. And she still felt guilty for it, but there was something else there too. She turned and gave Alice a very particular look that she couldn't quite read. "You think it was that other thing?" she asked.

Alice shook her head. She wasn't sure if she was catching this unspoken meaning properly, but she seemed to be trying to ask about the Bandersnatch. She met Sarah's eyes very carefully as she shook her head more forcefully. "No, that's not it," Alice told her.

Sarah looked satisfied, but Heather leaned in and looked between the two of them. "Not what?" Heather asked. "What do you two know about Nike?"

"That he's a little unstable," Sarah told Heather, putting both of her hands on Heather's shoulders and making her sit down on her bed. "It's nothing important. If it's not that, then it's not that. We need to come up with something else that might be after Alice. Or we could do something to get our minds off of it all together."

Heather let out a sigh. "Fine," she said. "But no flowers this time."

Sarah seemed happier at that one and she went to get her nail kit. Adrianna passed her a look and she mouthed the word *Bandersnatch* to her in explanation. Adrianna looked at her again and Alice shook her head no, it wasn't that this time. Alice didn't know who was coming after her. She hoped that it would let her at least get Adrianna's brothers out of Wonderland and not interfere with that.

While Sarah did their nails and made them much nicer than Alice had ever had them before, Heather kept trying to go down the list for options of who it could be. Alice let both of them do what they wanted, chatting along with them and turning down potential perpetrators as Heather came up with more outlandish motivations.

Alice fell asleep before anyone else, feeling herself drift off as she was sitting. All of this mess was very tiring and she had so much left to do. She was exhausted and her body took over for her, commanding her to get rest whether she wanted to or not.

CHAPTER 14

Culprits

THOUGH SHE DIDN'T need it, Alice gladly took the time off of school. There were people who knew who she was now that never knew her before. Her classmates wanted to talk to her, to offer her their sympathies or to tell her who was saying something about her behind her back. The extra attention alone made her uncomfortable and she was happier taking the week off from classes and letting Adrianna deal with it if she wanted to.

Alice went to the rooftop garden to get some solitude to work. There was a table there and no power, so she only had a little time alone with the book and a candle to cast enough fire over the page to see the notes in the margins. It was probably for the best, she thought, since it meant that she wouldn't be up here so long that people would worry that she'd disappeared again. They were paying far too much attention to her these days.

She had no idea how she was going to slip away. If people kept looking for her like this, she was never going to be able to just vanish for the long weekend. She hoped everyone was going to be heading home this year, but it was entirely unlikely and Alice was sure Adrianna couldn't cover for her this time around.

Still, she tried not to worry about that too much. She had to work out the Neverland version of the spell and her notes weren't quite as thorough as she thought they were on the topic of imagination. She had to go back through it, working out the new grammar structure and movements that went along with it. It was much easier now that she had some idea of how the people of Neverland worked, and she managed to rework how the Wonderland version went as well. With the new structure, it should work no matter where the hearts came from.

She was getting closer to finishing it all off. If she could just get Adam across, that might be enough. Adrianna would probably never forgive her completely for losing her other brother, but she barely noticed he was gone right now anyway. She would probably just let him fade away and Alice could hope Matt was happy wherever he'd ended up.

She closed the book and looked up to the November sky.

It was her half birthday today and she should do something to celebrate. She had managed to get not only a week's worth of homework done in a couple hours, but also figured out a complicated reworking of a spell that should work when she finally got around to trying it. Adrianna would teach her to say the words and everything would finally be done. One step closer to bringing Adam home.

She skimmed through the book again, not for the first or last time, trying to see if there was anything in there at all about making the Bandersnatch obey her. She needed to send it to Wonderland and, while there were little bits in here about making things do what you wanted them to, a lot of it had to do with much smaller and much less powerful things.

The green book next. There might be something that she could use. She might be able to convince him to go back to Wonderland on his own if she gave him just the right combination of herbs that, as near as she could figure, didn't actually exist. She had no idea how useful anything outside of the candlelight would be for her, but she also wasn't sure how much she could actually use what was in the candlelight either.

When she was happy with her progress she picked up her things. She put the red book away first, letting her hand run over the Mad Hatter's hat as she put it away. She needed to get him back and return that this weekend, whether or not she could cover up her disappearance. She put her computer back on her desk as well and stayed out in the cold just a little longer, trying to get all of her notes together. She put the finalized version of the spell in her pocket and wondered what she should do with the rest of these pages.

She couldn't let someone find them. She'd put these in her desk before, but that was careless. She couldn't keep shoving things in the ceiling, though. She didn't really need the notes anymore now that she had the important stuff written out on the computer and the finalized spell in her pocket.

Alice proceeded to set each page on fire, letting the small stream of smoke head up into the air and the pages burning on the table, blowing out the candle once she had lit all the pages. If the spell didn't work, she probably couldn't use these notes again anyway. She would start from scratch until she could figure out the right way.

"So this is where you hide every day," Peter's voice came above her. Alice dropped in her seat as he flew down to sit on the table, looking at the things she was burning. "That better not be important."

"It's not anymore," Alice said. "I hope not, anyway. What are you doing up here?"

"I thought someone was trying to send a smoke signal," Peter said, sounding a little sad about it. "It's been so long since I've seen one that was actually a signal." He drifted off for a moment before his attention snapped back to her. "Oh, and Adrianna is looking for you. But you're not going to go see her this time. Really bad idea."

Alice looked him over carefully. "Why?" she asked, keeping her eyes and voice very level.

"She said her brothers wanted to talk to you. The ones in the high school."

"Yeah," Alice said. She'd gotten enough email from Lori to know why. "My sister wants me to visit them to let them know I'm fine so they can tell her. I've been putting it off, but I really should."

"Nope," Peter said. "They're the ones that did it."

"Did what?"

"Broke into your room."

Alice narrowed her eyes at him, trying to figure out what his angle was. "How do you figure?" she asked, leaning forward to watch the paper turned ash in front of her.

"It was obviously them," Peter said. "We saw them when they were leaving, right? Why are high school students in a middle school?"

"Because they're Adrianna brothers," Alice told him. "They have a sibling in the dorms. Sometimes they visit."

"Really?" Peter sounded genuinely surprised.

"Of course," Alice told him, though it struck her that they actually never had come by as far as she could remember. Evan had when she first arrived, but no other time to visit Adrianna. They must have come by before for the triplets. They probably visited more than she remembered.

"I still don't trust them," Peter said. "All of that family smells funny."

"If she's looking for me, I should go where I can be found," Alice said, getting up. "Don't get caught flying."

Alice walked away and appeared back in the dorms, dropping down onto one of the couches. She pulled a novel out of her room, one that they were supposed to do readings of for class, and waited for everyone to find her. It shouldn't be hard from here, since this was precisely where she was yesterday when they went looking for her after class.

She got through two pages before they walked in with what felt like the rest of the school, all glad to be out of classes for the weekend. Reading break was upon them now and there were more than a few people who rushed upstairs to immediately change into things that were less school appropriate. Her friends came to sit with her, dropping their bags and looking frazzled.

"So much homework!" Robert told her as he sat down. "This is going to be the worst break."

"I'm already done," Alice said, smiling back at him sweetly. Her good mood would not be daunted. She had finally figured out how to fix the Neverland folk and she was getting closer to getting Adam back. All she had to do now was head back over and put the Mad Hatter's heart back.

"Can I see?"

Sarah smacked him for her, shaking her head disapprovingly. "You're doing your own homework."

"Ow!" Robert said. "Kidding!" He looked back at Alice briefly and shook his head like he wasn't actually.

Alice smiled and looked at Adrianna, who was shifting in her seat and on her phone, frantically sending texts back and forth. "Hey Adrianna?" she asked, drawing her attention. "Peter said you were looking for me."

"Peter?" Kevin asked.

"Yeah, he came by before you guys got here."

Kevin looked at her sideways, trying to decipher the lie out of her words. "Wasn't he heading out towards the gym?" Kevin asked both Heather and Alice, looking for some kind of confirmation. He didn't look pleased, like he was going to need to talk to that kid, but Alice ignored it.

Alice shrugged. "He popped by for a second," she said. "What's up?"

"Joe and Travis want to talk," Adrianna said. "Since we're homeless. They want to make sure we're okay. You want to meet them for dinner?"

"Sure," she said. "I'm ready whenever you want to go."

"Okay," Adrianna said. "Let me get changed. I think Lance is coming too."

"You guys have a whole family thing going on, don't you?" Sarah said. "Come on, I'll let you back in and fix you up. Alice, you too."

"I'm good," Alice said, letting Adrianna and Sarah leave without her and head back up to the room. Staying with Heather and Sarah for a few days had been nice. Sarah had insisted on making sure they looked their best every morning with a wide assortment of makeup that she got from her mother and, while Alice was not going to be seeing as many people, she still kept the colour on her face. It was just enough to make her look better than ever before.

"So when are you finally showing up for class again?" Kevin asked.

"I have to come back after the break," Alice told him. "Has everyone stopped talking about it yet?"

"About how you have some jealous boyfriend that you've never mentioned now coming after you for dumping him?" Kevin asked. "Seriously, with you not around, the rumours are getting out of hand. People think that Cat's come back after he found out about you and Nike a year ago to get his revenge."

"I wonder if I can get a little more time off," Alice muttered.

"Still no idea who it is?"

Alice shook her head. "I don't know anyone who I pissed off enough to do that. I'm hoping that whoever it was didn't realize what room they were in. Maybe he's after the person who used to be in the room and it has nothing to do with me at all. It's not like I go around making a lot of people mad at me."

"I know I'd feel a lot better if you at least knew how to defend yourself," Heather said. "I mean, that's twice now that you've narrowly missed someone coming in and trashing your room. And who knows how many times they've gone in there otherwise."

"Otherwise?"

"Heather's worried over nothing," Alice said, eyeing her and pleading with her to drop it.

"So it was more often," Robert said. "You know, I kind of figured. I mean, whoever it was, he had to be able to actually get into the room quick, right? So he's probably been scoping the place out for a while. And he's probably had to make a set of keys or something."

"Or the window," Heather said. "It's only the second floor."

"You guys don't really think that someone's got it out for me, do you?" Alice asked.

"You don't?" Heather demanded of her. "I don't know if

you've noticed, but you seem to attract all of the weird stuff. You go missing, sometimes for days, and you are the only one I know who ever talked to that purple haired psychopath in first year. And you just forgive Sarah for going out with Nike!"

"I didn't really want to go out with Nike in the first place," Alice pointed out.

"And wasn't there a thing last year?" Kevin asked.

Robert's eyes narrowed as he looked at Kevin. "Thing?"

Alice was glad for the distraction. Kevin shook it off and retracted the statement with a gesture and a few words. Not even Adrianna remembered that she had been missing for that month since the Bandersnatch worked his magic, but Kevin still seemed to retain something of whatever happened. Him and Sarah, who would very carefully avoid eye contact whenever he mentioned anything strange.

Alice was dragging a lot more people into the mess of her life than she should. But it would be all right. Middle school would be crazy, but with her gone in high school, their lives would be wiped clean of her. They could at least lead normal lives once that was all done with and she was gone.

She spotted Adrianna heading down the stairs and threw her book into her backpack, swinging it up onto her shoulder and making her exit as quick as she could before they remembered anything else she'd done. "It's been fun," Alice said. "I'll see you guys later tonight."

She fell in step beside Adrianna, glad to be outside, even if it was starting to rain. They stayed close to the building to avoid the raindrops, though Alice didn't even mind the weather. It meant the ashes of her notes would be washed away before they somehow managed to set the wet rooftop garden on fire.

"They seem really worried about us," Adrianna said, looking down at her phone as she kept texting. Alice glimpsed over and saw that the contact she was talking to wasn't Joe or Travis or Lance, but she didn't want to pry. "I think Lance told them you were taking the rest of the week off of classes."

"I haven't seen him at all lately," Alice noted, finding it strange now that she thought about it.

"He is in high school now," Adrianna said. "You get really busy there, I think."

"It's so weird not having him around all the time," Alice said. "Although it feels like we haven't even seen each other in forever."

"You don't want to come hang out much," Adrianna said. "You're always reading those books and going off to Wonderland on the weekends. You're so busy."

Alice nodded, knowing that it was true. She was very wrapped up in everything that was going on, only showing up for study sessions and none of the fun stuff these days. "Sorry," she said. "I just really need to get Adam out soon and I think I'm getting close."

"Really?" Adrianna asked, sounding a little more excited at that. "He's actually going to come back?"

"Hopefully," Alice said. "I think that maybe if I can get the Mad Hatter back and finish off whatever his plan is, Adam might finally come back. Then I just need to find Matt and everything I did will be better. That way, if I never figure out this Bandersnatch thing, at least you'll have your brothers back."

"You're going to figure out the Bandersnatch thing," Adrianna said. "I'm sure that he'll let you go if he sees that you tried really hard. Have you asked?"

"I don't think it's going to work that way," Alice said. "But maybe if I can look at the brown book again, I might be able to come up with something. There might be notes on there that I didn't get to see before that can tell me how to make him do what I want him to."

"Maybe he'll let you borrow it," Adrianna said. "Or maybe he'll let you read it while you're there."

"Maybe." Alice forced herself to smile at that one, though the thought of willingly going into the Bandersnatch's lair just to read the book that she hoped to use to make him van-ish left her cold. She had already come to terms with the fact that it would be a lot easier to just let herself fade away instead of holding out hope that she could stumble into a solution, despite the ideas that occasionally ran through her head.

"What *is* happening in Wonderland?" she asked, lowering her voice and checking around for people listening. With the rain, outdoors was sparsely populated despite the start of the long weekend and Alice could tell they were not going to get many people listening in.

"Well," Alice said, realizing she hadn't actually given Adrianna an update at all, "a lot. The Queen of Hearts couldn't take the hearts from the people from Neverland — Well, she could, but they kept holding onto them — so she stopped going after them, I think. Adam and Tiger Lily managed to get a lot of them into the White Rabbit's house. But now the Queen managed to get the Mad Hatter's heart and he was taking a bunch of people out to where the tear to Neverland is, so I convinced them to go to the White Rabbit's house instead. And now they're trying to get his heart back while I try to figure out how to get the hearts back into the people in Neverland."

"Wow," Adrianna said.

"We trapped the Mad Hatter just on the weekend," Alice said. "I need to go back tonight or tomorrow and see if they have his heart and to see if this thing I did for Neverland works."

"I wish I could help," Adrianna said. "It sounds like a lot of stuff."

"I got it," Alice said. "Adam's helping too on the other side. And Tiger Lily doesn't hate me anymore, so that's helpful. It's not like I'm doing everything all on my own. And you're here to help me make sure I remember homework and keep me company when bad things happen. So what's the plan for the night?"

"They wanted to try some restaurant off campus," Adrianna said. "We're just going to meet up with everyone in Joe and Travis' room and then we'll head out to wherever it is."

Alice let Adrianna lead her through the dorms up to their brothers' room and knocked on the door. Alice remembered the last time she was there, huddling in the corner, and when the door swung open it was much the same as she remembered it. It even had the same smell as before. Joe was the one that got up to answer the door, letting them both in and closing the door behind them.

"So how's being homeless?" he asked as they came in. Lance was sitting on Travis' bed as Travis got his shoes on and they looked up, ushering the girls to take a seat on Joe's bed as Joe went back to his laptop. The soft, familiar sound of Lori's music drifted through the room.

"Not homeless," Adrianna said. "Sarah and Heather took us in."

"I swear, as soon as I leave then everything goes wrong," Lance said. "Who the hell did you piss off, Alice?"

"No one!" Alice insisted. "They probably just have the wrong room. I haven't done anything to anyone to make them this mad at me."

"But you have done *something*," Lance said, casting a brief glance at the mirror. He smiled and seemed to think he had it figured out as much as he could and didn't bother asking anything more. Alice tried not to let it show on her face, but he was probably right at this point.

"I wonder if that ghost is back again," Travis said, grinning at Joe. Joe picked up the headphones off his desk and threw them at him, Travis catching them and tossing them back.

"No pissing off ghosts," Joe said, pointing his headphones at her before putting them back down again. "I am not dealing with that shit again."

"You loved it," Travis said, still laughing.

"I know where you sleep."

"You do know that."

"I could murder you."

"You could."

"I'm not covering your dinner."

"Now that's just cruel."

Travis got up and led the way to the door, the rest of them falling in line. The sound of several phones **receiving** several texts all at once distracted them. Alice ignored it, getting to her feet herself and adjusting her coat around her, only to realize that something was strange. For one thing, the music was louder.

Alice looked up and Joe was at his computer, turning the volume up. Behind her, Travis stood at the door, not moving or taking his hand off the handle or eyes off of his phone. It was like he had been frozen in time and Joe didn't look like he was moving either. He blinked, like he knew there was something wrong, but he couldn't figure out what it was.

Adrianna turned around slowly and from there, Alice knew something was very wrong. She'd never seen Adrianna so blank-faced before, or seen her drop her phone to the ground so casually. She took Alice by both arms and held them, squeezing her nails into Alice's forearm.

"Adrianna?" she asked, trying to gently pull her arms out of her grip. Adrianna was much stronger than she gave her credit for, her nails scratching into Alice's arms and not letting her go no matter how much she tried to pull away. "Adrianna, what's wrong?" she asked, looking wildly back at Travis, who still did nothing. If he wasn't looking back yet, he wasn't going to help. "Adrianna, you're hurting me. Let go! Adrianna!"

Behind her, she could feel someone stepping in. Something wrapped around her neck, something long and slender, and pulled her back into them. She tilted back, seeing Lance there, just as empty faced as Adrianna.

She couldn't even bring herself to make a noise, everything being choked out by the thing around her neck biting into her skin. She needed to get out of there, to escape, but even if she wanted to vanish, she couldn't with Adrianna's nails digging into her arms and holding her with more strength than Alice knew she had.

She threw herself to the side, knocking them off balance and into the bed. She managed to duck out from whatever Lance had around her neck. She pulled one of her arms out of Adrianna's hands, trying to make it for the door. Heaving a breath into her lungs, she managed to reach past Travis before the coughing took her and Adrianna pulled her back towards her. She tried to pull away, but her whole body hurt from trying to breathe. She forced herself to keep moving, but Travis turned and he was much larger than his sister. She flinched away on reflex, looking for another way out.

Alice turned around and dove forward at the mirror. Wonderland. She wasn't going to get to the door, but she might be able to get to Wonderland and away from them. She felt something catch around her neck as she dove forward, Adrianna grabbing her by the leg and Alice fell forward into the floor of the White Rabbit's house, hoping that they would not follow.

She knew that they had.

CHAPTER 15

Guests in Wonderland

ALICE'S FACE HIT the floor of the White Rabbit's house, but it did not stay there long. There was a knee in her back as the slender rope around her neck was pulled taught and yanked her backwards, cutting into her throat. There was something pinning her legs down, but she kicked back, trying to gain her balance and grab at the rope cutting off her air. She couldn't get her balance, couldn't get a grip, couldn't breathe.

Spots covered her vision as her mind started to go fuzzy. She knew she had to focus, but panic flooded her thoughts, needing to get away from this. She needed to *breathe*. She kicked, the weight finally getting off her legs and she thought she heard something shatter, but the knee in her back didn't move and the rope around her neck showed no sign of slackening. She tried getting under the rope, but it was flat against her neck and she couldn't find a space that her fingers could slip through. She couldn't get a grip, the rope more a part of her neck than her skin.

Everything was getting dark and she couldn't even feel the fingers scratching at her neck anymore. She wasn't sure if she was even trying, or only thought she was.

Her face smacked into the ground and the weight was off her back. With nothing pulling her backwards or keeping her down, she curled into herself and kept pulling at her throat. Finally, she pulled the string away from it. The air burned her throat as it gave her life. She felt light headed as it filled her lungs, but for the moment there was nothing better, even as it started to escape as coughs that she could feel in her bones.

She looked up through bleary eyes over one of the bodies to see Adam there, pinning Lance down on the ground. Lance struggled, but Adam had him firmly pinned to the ground between the bodies.

"*What the fuck do you think you're doing?*" Adam demanded. "Keep moving and I'm going to knock you out!"

Lance continued to move, wriggling one hand free of Adam's grasp. Adam took something out of his belt and clocked Lance hard across the back of the head. Lance went still under him.

"Alice of Wonderland, is there anyone who does not try to kill you?" Tiger Lily asked. Alice looked up, still coughing too hard to even push herself up, and saw that Tiger Lily was holding Adrianna limply at her side, her roommate now unconscious.

Alice desperately tried to get enough breath into herself make the coughing stop, but found that someone much more fluffy was willing to help. The White Rabbit picked her up off the floor and deposited her on the couch to continue coughing and shaking out of the way. Adam waved at Tiger Lily to set Adrianna down next to him so he could get a better look at her before turning his attention back to Alice on the couch. He did not get off of his brother.

"What happened?" Adam asked Alice as the coughing fits started to subside. "I mean, Lance might take a swing at you if you tried to kill him first, but he's not going to actually try to kill you. And I've never seen Addie get mad enough to... well, get mad in the first place. She used to talk back, but she's not the type to do *that* to you."

"You know these two," Tiger Lily said.

Adam smiled a tired smile and leaned back on Lance. "Ah, you haven't met my family," he said. "This over here is my little sister, Adrianna. You know the one that's not up to hurting anything, even if it's coming at her with a knife? And this is the smart brother, Lance."

"You keep poor company, Alice of Wonderland."

Alice shook her head, still trying to make her throat feel less like something had been cutting into it. She still breathed raggedly and she wanted nothing more than to lay down for a few hours and wait for this nightmare to blow over. Even lying down, everything felt like it was moving.

"I don't know what happened," Alice croaked out, feeling like her throat was still trying to get back to its old shape. She coughed out the last of her words, letting herself fall silent and trying to make her head and the world stop spinning around her. She rubbed at her arms. The punctures from Adrianna's fingernails still stung.

Tiger Lily looked over both of them and took in a strange, derisive sniff. "They smell strange," Tiger Lily said, going to the pouch at her side that she carried and pulling out two sprigs of something. She put one in Adrianna's mouth and passed the other one to Adam who didn't hesitate to do the same to Lance.

"I need to take them back," Alice said, trying to stand up and coughing harder from the movement. The White Rabbit pushed her back down, though Alice protested. "They can't—"

"You cannot stand on your own feet," Tiger Lily said. "You will not be taking them anywhere."

Alice relented under the White Rabbit's hand and lay back down. She was still trembling and so dizzy. Why did she feel so weak? "They need to go back..."

"You should learn to trust your nose, Alice of Wonderland," Tiger Lily said harshly, gently shaking Adrianna back awake. "You can smell the taint of something on them."

"Peter said something about that," Alice muttered. She felt much better lying down, she had to admit. The world didn't spin quite the same and she felt like she was breathing better down here. "What did you give to them?"

"It will bring them back to themselves," Tiger Lily said. "I would kill them, but they are friends of yours and family of his. I will respect that. I am still very much trying to repay my debt to you, Alice of Wonderland, and this is only a small token. I assure you, I will do much more."

Alice nodded and watched as Adrianna started to stir. Adam turned Lance over and took a seat on his chest, smacking him hard across the face. Lance was up quickly, trying to sit up and finding himself pinned. He struggled for exactly as long it took for him to look up and see his own face looking down at him.

"Adam?" Lance asked, not believing his eyes. "It's been a year! Where the hell have you been?"

"Not trying to kill girls," Adam told him. "You want to explain yourself?"

"I…" Lance trailed off, his head drooping to the side to look at where he was. There were bodies all across the floor, curled up with bloody hearts in their hands and holes in their chests where those hearts had been removed from. He went very still and his face paled. "Where am I?" he asked in a very small voice.

"Nope," Adam told him, grabbing him by the face with one hand and turning his head back up to face him. "You are going to tell me why you decided to try and kill Alice."

Adrianna groaned beside them and turned toward the wall.

"I tried to..." Lance's face screwed up as he strained to remember. "But I wouldn't..."

"With a shoelace," Adam said, moving his hand up to Lance's forehead and pinning his head down with his palm so that he couldn't turn it.

"With... oh god! I did. I— What was I— Is she okay?"

Adam took his hand off of his head and pointed him to Alice lying down on the couch. Alice didn't bother trying to get up or move, feeling very comfortable with the world not spinning around at the moment. A small cough escaped her and her laboured breathing echoed in the quiet room.

"What happened?" Lance asked. "Why— Can you get off me already?"

"You going to keep yourself from killing Alice?"

Lance glowered up at him. "I can't promise the same for you if you don't get off."

Adam got up off of him and offered him a hand to get

back to his feet. "So you and Addie just went nuts and tried to kill her?"

"I don't know what happened," Lance said. "I tried to kill her with a shoelace. I took a shoelace out of my shoe."

"If you could hold off until we have this little situation here settled before you make another attempt on her life—" Adam gestured at the bodies around them "—that would be appreciated. We still kind of need her over here, though. Just for, you know, a few more months. Maybe years."

"I didn't mean to try and kill her!"

"Sure," Adam said, kneeling down to see Adrianna. "Just that you almost did. And at the worst time, because we have a small army plus the Queen of Hearts on the way over here to dig up the Mad Hatter and we can't find his heart anywhere."

"I'm sure it is located somewhere in anywhere," the White Rabbit said. He got a glass of water ready and brought it back over to Alice, bounding over the bodies in his living room. "If it was nowhere, then we would be in quite a bit of trouble. Anywhere is simply vast, not impossible."

"So it's Wonderland," Lance said flatly. "What's with the guys on the floor with their hearts out?"

"Neverland," Adam said, Tiger Lily going to Alice's side with the water and helping her sit while the boys tried to revive their sister. "If you take someone's heart out and they aren't from Wonderland, this is what happens. Or, at least, if they're from Neverland. I don't think Alice or I have had our heart out yet to find out what happens to us. You?"

"Almost," Lance said, clearly unsettled by the people around him, though Adam was comfortable around them now. They were like unfortunate cushions that had been laid out on the floor. Or cats playing with yarn, if that yarn were still beating hearts. "I am so happy I got out of that."

"I'll get you back," Alice said hoarsely. She was still rocking forward in her seat and it was hard for her to get her words out. Tiger Lily looked disapprovingly on and forced Alice to continue drinking as she tended to her arms and tried to get a better look at the bloody red gash around her neck. "Travis and Joe are going to notice. You need to get back."

"Can you even stand up?" Lance asked. He leaned toward her for a moment before he became very busy concentrating on bringing Adrianna around.

"She cannot," Tiger Lily told him, pushing Alice back down onto the couch when she tried. "You shouldn't attempt to strangle her again. Next time, I'll take your head."

"She won't," Adam told him. "Well, unless I piss her off and she thinks I'm you."

"That's happened a few too many times for me to be comforted by that," Lance said. "What did you say about the Queen of Hearts coming here?"

"Right, you were in her house for a while, weren't you?" Adam said. "Where does she keep the good hearts? Do you know? I have been trying to find them and it has been driving me nuts. We tried the throne, but we can't find the right one."

"I don't think this is the time," Lance said. "If the Queen of Hearts is on her way, we have to get out of here. She's a little screwy and I seem to remember she has a special thing for Alice."

"*Everyone* around here has a special thing for Alice," Adam told him. "She is the most popular person in Wonderland in that everyone either wants her dead or thinks she is the rudest creature to ever walk the planet. It is legitimately impressive."

"Yeah, I remember that part too," Lance said. "I have no idea how she does it."

Adrianna let out a noise as she got to her upright position, looking around and seeing her two brothers standing over her. She stared wide-eyed at one, then the other, then back at one again before she leapt up and caught him around the neck. "Adam!" she said. "You're okay!"

"And Alice said you guys didn't care that I was gone," he said, smiling. "Long time."

"Alice..." Adrianna said, her eyes glazing over as she tried to remember what happened. "Oh my god!" she said as the realization dawned on her. "I did something! I don't know how, but, oh no..." she said, looking down at her hands. She saw the bits of blood under her fingernails and looked back up to both of them, her eyes settling on Lance. "We didn't, did we?"

Lance looked embarrassed, looking away before he nodded silently. He said nothing.

"You both *did* try to kill her," Adam said. "That wasn't very nice."

"I wasn't trying to kill her," Adrianna insisted. "I was just supposed to keep her from going anywhere. Because she can do the... Where are we? What— What are those?" she asked, noticing the people on the ground all curled around their hearts. Her eyes went wide and she backed away from them. "Are they dead?"

"It's okay," Adam said, looking hesitantly back at the bodies as Lance tried very hard not to look at them at all. "They're not dead they're just... Okay, sleeping is the wrong word, but they aren't dead. They just had... did Alice tell you anything? Do you know anything about Wonderland?"

"We're in Wonderland?" Adrianna asked, her eyes going wide and narrow and wide again as she looked around at the house. "I don't know if I like it here."

Adam let out a laugh. "You haven't even talked to anyone yet," he said. "But they're okay. Alice is working on a way to get their hearts back inside them so that they can be good as new and not.... this."

"Is she okay?" Adrianna asked. "We did such awful things to her. I don't know if she's going to be okay after that. She'll probably never forgive us for it."

"You'll be fine," Adam told her, looking back at Alice as she started to regain her strength. "She just needs a minute to catch her breath. Lance was yanking on the laces a little harder than he should have been."

Alice smiled and stayed quiet, looking out the window and letting her eyes trail across the garden outside. There was no sign of anything out there except for something moving in the distance. A very large number of somethings that were very slowly coming closer.

She waved and caught Tiger Lily by the arm, pointing out the approaching mob outside. Tiger Lily rose to her feet and nodded at Adam, walking around the house and picking up her more deadly implements that she'd left around. "Adam, we have no more time."

Adam nodded and turned to his siblings. "You guys are going to want to stay in here," he told them.

"Are you going to be in trouble?"

"No more than usual." Adam smiled.

Adrianna frowned at him, but Lance glanced out the window. The Queen of Hearts could be seen through the milling of other bodies around her. "She apparently keeps the really important things on her at all times," Lance told him. "Someone told me that there was a shelf under her skirt once. I've seen her pull cutlery out of there before, but... You know what, if you're looking for an important heart, it's probably in there."

"You're kidding me."

Lance offered a smile and a shrug, pulling Adrianna away from the window deeper into the house.

Alice rose, looking back at the pair of them. "I'll get you out of here," she said, feeling steadier on her feet now. Her voice was still hoarse, but she could move a little more. Her neck and arms stung, but that wasn't important right now. With the Queen of Hearts on the way, she had to get them both out of here as quickly as she could.

"No you aren't," Adam said, pointing to where the mirror used to be. "You kicked Addie into it. We'll get this settled and then we'll find you a new mirror. Sit tight."

"You need help," Alice said.

"Not from you," Adam told her putting a hand on her shoulder. "Relax. Tiger Lily and I got this."

"You don't." She could see in Adam's eyes that he was just putting on a good show for his siblings, but he had no idea what he was going to do. He stared down at her, head tilting and looking at her like she needed to stop talking right now, but it was clear that he didn't have a plan.

Alice let her eyes drift around the room. "Give me a few

minutes," she said quietly, eyes lingering on a few of the hearts around the room before she let her gaze drift back to him, a small smile playing on her lips. "I'll be along in a few minutes. Stall until then."

Adam nodded and followed Tiger Lily outside after the White Rabbit, who thought it was time to water his garden of hands. The Mad Hatter was still nowhere in sight, but Alice had other things to worry about right now.

She turned back to the rest of the room and took a deep, shaky breath. A cough rose in her throat, but she managed to keep it down and she kept her eyes level on the bodies around her. A plan. She had a plan.

"Adrianna," Alice said, taking a piece of paper out of her pocket. "I need a hand."

"You don't look so good," Adrianna said. She was very careful not to get too close to any of the bodies as she pulled herself away from Lance and came closer. "I'm so sorry. I didn't mean to—"

"It's fine," Alice told her. "I just need to know how to pronounce this properly. You can apologize later, but right now, we need to make sure they aren't going to... to get really hurt out there."

Adrianna sat with Alice on the couch and went through the words, Alice picking them up very quickly this time. They had been through enough similar words before that Alice was almost used to the pronunciation by now. There were only a few kinks to work through, no more than a minute spent on them, before she thought she had the words down.

"What's it for?" Lance asked, watching as Alice very carefully chose a Native man on the ground to kneel in front of. "What are you doing?"

"Helping," Alice said. She let herself relax, not thinking about any of the parts of her that stung or wanted to cough or curl up and lie down again, replacing those thoughts with the need to be whole. She became very aware of her heart and where it was in her body and how much she needed it there. Her heart was in there like a magnet stitched together with ideas and thoughts.

She put her hands on the backs of the man's hands and let those feelings flow out of her and into him. Her mouth moved, the words coming out over and over again, gently coaxing him to pull his heart back into himself. In her mind, she drew that line between his mind and his heart, connecting them from inside and tugged the heart closer.

The heart left his hand and drifted back into place in his chest. Alice waited until she could feel the connection before she put her hand on the hole, trying to seal it before the heart could escape. The hole closed up much more quickly than she thought it would. She wasn't even tired and felt like she could do a few more of them if she needed to.

And she would need to.

The man opened his eyes and jumped to his feet, staring down at Alice with a knife in his hand. Adrianna gasped and Lance held her in place with a hand clamped over her mouth. Alice put up her hands quickly, ignoring them and keeping her eyes on the man. "Hello," she said. "I'm Alice. I put your heart back."

He looked around, eyes widening at the sight of so many bodies littered around them, people he seemed to recognize holding their hearts in their hands. "What is this place?" he asked.

"The Queen of Hearts is coming here. Tiger Lily is outside now to stop her from reaching here. Will you help us?"

"Prove that you do what you say you do, Alice, and I may. Heal him."

Alice nodded calmly and went to another Native man, repeating the process under the gaze of a man whose knife had yet to be put away. She was calm under the pressure and she managed to get his heart in again, this time only feeling a little winded from the effort. When the man rose, this time with an axe in his hands to strike her, the first man stopped him and pulled him aside. He pointed out a woman to revive next.

The first man directed the second outside to follow Tiger Lily while Alice worked, though Alice was growing tired by the fifth. The first knelt down to her when he saw her breathing more heavily at the sixth body and put a gentle hand on her arm to pull her back.

"If it is the Queen of Hearts out there, Alice, we will also need a witch at our side. Do not tire."

Alice nodded getting to her feet. "I'll need a minute to catch my breath," she told him. "Try not to kill anyone. Tell Tiger Lily I'll be there in a minute."

The man nodded and left, heading into the woods and leaving Alice there to take a seat on the couch. Her eyes drifted out the window at what was happening. Adrianna and Lance were already sitting at the glass again, their eyes darting between watching Alice work and what was going on outside.

"What's going on?" Alice asked.

"It's too far away," Adrianna said. "I can't see anything."

"I'll get a closer look," Alice said, getting up.

Lance grabbed her before she could get away. "Are you sure?" he asked. "You really don't look so good."

Alice glanced back at the broken mirror. "I have to," she said. "Just this one thing. And then we'll get you guys back home."

She was gone before they could stop her, taking a seat in the tree overlooking the confrontation, which was only getting started. The White Rabbit was talking while Tiger Lily and the other Natives were nowhere to be seen. She was sure they were there, but Alice didn't know where. The flash of metal from the bushes gave her an idea, though it wasn't until she saw a flash of Tiger Lily that she knew for certain.

"So you see, it's very rude to attempt to enter the property of someone without obeying the rules of the person whose property it is," the White Rabbit was saying.

"I am the Queen!" the Queen of Hearts bellowed at him. "I own all of this land!"

"Ah, but this house happens to be my castle, of which I am King," the White Rabbit informed her. "And as a King, I believe that trumps a Queen, Madam of Hearts. I would like to kindly request you leave my property and my kingdom."

"Bring him here," the Queen of Hearts snapped to the blank playing card immediately behind her. "I require his heart, if only to shut him up."

The card stepped forward, drawing his sword and pointing it at the White Rabbit. Alice flinched forward, though Adam was quicker, catching the sword with his knife and pushing it down as he stepped in close. He shook his head, a smile on his face as if he were looking forward to this.

"No taking anyone today," he said, his hand moving quickly and twisting the sword out of the card's hand until it was in his own. He kicked the card away and looked back to the queen with a smile. "I'm afraid you heard the Rabbit," he said. "He doesn't want you here."

"So the false king has a false knight as well," the Queen of Hearts said, her mouth curled up in a sneer. She waved two more forward to Adam. "This travel has been tiresome and I am in desperate need of amusement. You shall entertain me until I am content, and then I shall have both of your hearts."

"My pleasure," Adam said, twisting the knife in one hand to a better grip and taking the fight head on. Alice got the distinct impression that he was enjoying himself and she was almost certain that he didn't need her help in the matter. He was quick enough to avoid getting hit and was a more than capable fighter. In fact, Alice thought he might be pulling his punches.

The Natives had disappeared from the bushes near the front line, though they were not gone. They were in the back, silently picking off the troop one man at a time. They were pulled into the forest to never return, one by one.

Alice did her part from where she was to keep everyone safe. She reached forward, her hand appearing at the side of one of the soldiers and grabbed hold of the sword at his side. She pulled it back towards her and stuck it into the tree before she reached for the next one. None of them thought to look when she took them, all the men very carefully trained not to move unless their queen allowed it. And their Queen was too busy enjoying the battle in front of her.

It was a yell from somewhere near the house that made

Adam look away at the wrong moment. Alice heard it too, but her attention was stuck on the events in front of her, and where Adam was tripped, falling to his knees and with two swords crossed at his throat.

The White Rabbit ran back to the house, but the Queen hardly cared. "Run for now, Rabbit, but I will have stew tonight and I do very much enjoy rabbit."

The Queen of Hearts advanced on Adam, smiling broadly as she got close enough to him. "You have pleased your Queen," she said. "For that, you will be allowed into my service." Her smile curved a little too large and Alice could see that Tiger Lily was too far away to know what was happening.

"Do you really want him, though?" Alice asked, appearing at the Queen's side and looking down at Adam. "He doesn't look like a terribly good specimen. Not in good shape at all."

The Queen looked to her and the sneer returned to her face. "I remember you, child," she said. "The tricky one that the Cheshire Cat wanted to give me as a daughter. You appear to be in even worse condition than before. That anyone would ever think you would be an appropriate child is laughable."

"And I see you unmelted pretty well," Alice said, smiling. "I do remember a time when you were asking me to be your daughter, though. That I would do well at your side. I must say, though, your side is a bit uncomfortable. I think I made an excellent choice in turning you down. You still smell like the Jabberwocky's flame and I think I can even see where you melted before."

"You insolent child!" she snapped at her, Adam forgotten. "Hold her. I will have her heart first."

Alice stepped around the Queen of Hearts and appeared around the side of one of the men holding Adam. "That's not very nice," Alice said. She moved again as the men closed in on her, over to the side of the other man. When they came for her again, she went back to the Queen's side, watching as they tripped over one another to get to her.

Adam slipped away, looking back to the house. They exchanged a look and Alice nodded. She would deal with this here while he went to see what was happening and that everything was alright.

"How can this many people have so much trouble stopping a small girl?" Alice asked the Queen, looking up at her with her head tilted to one side. "I do believe you need a better team with you, your highness. This is silly."

"Off with her head!" she screeched at them. They continued to mob toward her, Alice laughing as she stepped farther away.

The laugh was a bad idea. One caught in her throat and her body protested in the form of a cough. They started small at first, but that was all they needed to be to distract her. She didn't watch where she was going, and the blank cards were upon her. She didn't know if she fell first or if they knocked her over, but she had fallen and was swallowed up by the darkness of a deck of falling cards.

CHAPTER 16

Many Boxes

"HAS SHE TOLD you about this Bandersnatch thing? At the end of the school year, she's apparently just going to disappear. I'm thinking that on top of everything else is why she's so—"

"Wait, disappear?"

"Like, Evan disappear. If she hasn't hit her limit yet, she's going to very soon. And that's bad news for everyone over here. We need her in good shape like you wouldn't believe. I've been trying to keep her on your side thinking it might be a bit better over there. Keep her from being too stressed out."

"Addie said she's been a bit distracted all semester. After everything else that's been happening to her, I'm a little surprised that she hasn't cracked already."

"You mean besides you trying to kill her?"

"Oh, would you lay off on that?"

Alice stirred. Something was clamped into her leg. It felt like it was biting into her ankle as she stirred and it stung with every movement. The chain rattled and she went very still, trying to focus instead on just how much her head was hurting. She let out a soft groan, regretting the return to consciousness.

"How about not this time?" Adam suggested. "Unless you're *really* sure it never happened before and it's not going to happen again. Hey Alice, has Lance ever tried to kill you before?"

"No," she muttered.

"So at least there's that," Adam said.

"I think I broke into their room, though," Lance continued. In the dim light, Alice could see his brow furrow and his eyes went to his feet, currently in chains. He brought his knees up, his shackled hands going to his temples as he tried to concentrate. "When the power went out. The room was covered in glass and I scratched my hands up pretty good. I was looking for… something…"

"A book," Alice told him, though she was confused. "But I don't have the brown book anymore."

"No," Lance said, his head shaking, but his eyes not blinking or moving. "It was a green one. I needed to get a green book."

"I'm more curious about why your room was covered in glass," Adam said, looking back at Alice.

Alice frowned, barely thinking about it. "That was Peter," she said offhandedly bending down to see her leg. She found her arms shackled as well and let her hands disappear long enough for the metal clatter to the ground.

"Who's Peter?"

"Pan?"

Lance turned to his brother and raised an eyebrow, though Adam's attention was on Alice as she kept thinking.

"Yeah him," Alice said. "Green book? That's... oh."

"Oh?"

Alice let herself go slack against the wall as she put the pieces together. She got the green book from the weird room in Adrianna's house. It was obvious now that she thought about it who that room belonged to. Though she never saw Claudia while she was there this time, she knew there was something strange about her. She hadn't thought about that Christmas, but it felt like it made sense.

"Claudia," she said at last. "It's Claudia."

"What?" the boys said, both at the same time. Lance stared at her like she had gone crazy. Adam's head glanced around and he made a quick gesture to indicate that they needed to keep quiet.

Alice shook her head at their reaction. "She's not from

here," Alice said, keeping her voice down. "Well, not Wonderland, but not back home either. She might be from Neverland. And I found this book in your house in a sewing room, but when the light was off it didn't look like a sewing room at all. There were all these plants and stuff all over the place."

"You stole something from Claudia?" Lance asked, the blank look entering his eyes again. Adam looked at him and smacked him, the glaze falling off his eyes instantly.

"Okay, so maybe it's Claudia," Adam said. "She always seemed normal enough to me, but I've been wrong plenty of times before."

"What did you do that for?"

"I don't have any more of that plant stuff Tiger Lily carries, so I had to improvise."

"Improvise for what?"

Adam didn't answer and Alice let her attention wander to her surroundings. They were moving, that much she knew. They appeared to be inside a large metal box with several small holes at the very top. The sunlight crawled in to let them see just enough of what was inside. They were alone in there, all in chains, and Alice found just why her leg hurt so much.

"I can see if Alice can keep bringing that flower back for you," Adam told Lance. "There's a thing you can make out of it and you won't have to worry about the curse stuff anymore."

"What the hell are you talking about?"

"Where are we?" Alice asked. She frowned at the bear trap that bit into her calf. It stung, but she wasn't in too much pain from it. It just pierced her skin and kept her very firmly there, like the Cheshire Cat had with his claws before. She could handle this. The burn around her throat still stung more than the jaws on her leg.

"Why, lost of course," a silky voice said out of nowhere. Alice caught the eye of the Cheshire Cat and her shoulders dropped as she leveled a stare at his eyes, waiting for the rest of him to appear. She was displeased and her face told so. "Though lost is a particular specialty of yours. I think you will find yourself perfectly at home."

"Hello Cat," Alice said. "Why are you here?"

"Why, Alice, I am always here," Cat said smoothly, settling down on her leg. He sat on the trap on her leg and she let out a hiss as it bit deeper into her muscle. "Though here will always be a place that changes, I assure you that here is where I will always be if you ever need to find me."

"Don't sit there," Alice said, reaching over to move him off. Cat moved on his own, brushing up around her shoulders and settling down there with more weight than she was prepared for. She wavered under him and didn't turn to look at his face, though she could feel him curl closer around her neck and whisper in her ear.

"The Mad Hatter will die if you are not quick with your

escape," the Cheshire Cat said before slinking back off her shoulders. He slunk away and trotted back around to her lap as if he were expecting her to pet him.

"I must admit, though, this is a difficult place to be lost in," Cat said. "There isn't even a place for you to turn! Perhaps you have found a means to keep yourself from ever getting lost again! Though I don't know why you would want to. It was the one thing you are good at."

Alice looked long at Cat, trying to determine if he was serious. It sounded true, but also far too sane a statement. Still, she didn't want to take the risk. "I need this thing off my leg," she said, looking back and forth between the Case brothers. "One of you knows how to pick a lock."

Adam grinned and looked to Lance, who went over to get a better look at the lock on her leg. "I need two long pins or sticks or something that isn't going to break," he said. "Long as you can get them. And a light. And these things off my hands." He held up his shackles, finding that they were covering the entirety of his hands like Adam's were. "But there's nothing in here."

"You delight in surrounding yourself by people who are much less intelligent than you are, Alice," Cat said, looking back at Lance. "It is nearly as impressive as finding yourself a place that you cannot get lost in."

"Don't you have somewhere else to be?" Alice asked,

reaching behind her and thinking hard of two slender pins that she could use. Skewers came to mind, about the right size and very slender if they were being used right. She could come up with that easily, finding them in her hand and closing her fingers around them a moment later and she pulled them back out from behind her and handed them to Lance.

"How did you do that?" Lance asked, unable to take the needles from her yet. She dropped them in her lap and reached into the darkness, pulling in her hand a moment later with Lance's shackles in her hands. Confusion spread across his face.

"If you get my coat for me, I have some matches," Adam said. Alice pulled it out of the air as well and handed it back to him, Adam taking it. Alice wasn't sure how he had gotten free, but she found she wasn't surprised that he had found a way.

"You keep dull company," Cat said, taking his leave and vanishing again. "I suppose it reflects what you have become."

"What happened?" Alice asked as Lance got to work on her ankle. "I think I missed a lot."

"They came by and dug up the Mad Hatter," Lance told her as he started to work on the bear trap under the light of Adam's flame. "The White Rabbit wasn't that helpful and the plants got all messed up and started going crazy and letting everyone go. The Mad Hatter recognized you, Alice, and said he needed to get you and the hearts for his Queen. Adam tried to be a hero—"

"And it would have worked if this one didn't decide to get so freaked out by close calls," Adam said. "But now we're all in chains together in a box. At least Tiger Lily got Addie out of there."

"Why do we still have our hearts?" Alice asked, watching Lance work. "I figured the Queen would want them."

"That was Lance," Adam said. "Apparently we all know about other worlds full of people who haven't given her their heart yet, and if she takes ours she will never find out about it. So now we're in a box."

"Better a box than with our hearts out," Lance told him, his eyes not leaving the trap as he worked on it. "Have you figured out where we're going? I still can't make out what anyone's talking about and I don't really know this place. Well, not outside that castle."

Adam stared at him from behind the match. "I'm in the same box as you are."

"Probably to the edge of Wonderland," Alice said. "She got the Mad Hatter back, right? And Hatter was heading for Neverland. And if you remember anything Tiger Lily told you about Neverland, you know why that really can't happen."

"Because it's full of zombies?" Adam asked. "I thought you said that Matt might be in there."

"Matt would definitely be in there," Lance said. "He could fight zombies. Do you remember how much he wanted to fight zombies?"

Adam shook his head. "I went in there with Tiger Lily once to get some of that plant stuff," he said. "It's not fun. Trust me, it's *so* much nicer on this side with the crazy queen than whatever the hell is happening over there. It's nuts. It might also possibly be the only time I've seen night since I fell through that mirror."

"Why are you in a bear trap?" Lance asked as he got the trap unset and pulled it gently off of Alice's leg. He was unimpressed with the spikes that dug into her skin and was gentle as he could be, wincing as he saw the blood now dripping down her calf.

Alice brought her leg back under her and tried to stand. The box was just a little too short for her. "I'm going to get this open," Alice said. "Adam, can you handle things while I deal with the Mad Hatter?"

Adam nodded and Alice thought of the keys, finding them easily and grabbing hold of them. She appeared on the back of a horse behind a card.

It looked like they had stopped, many of them either sitting or standing about in the sparse underbrush. Alice could see the Piccaninny's village through the sparse trees, putting them just at the edge of the forest. Looking the other way, she could see into the clearing where the Queen of Hearts insisted on having a cup of tea and put her feet up on an obedient, heartless beaver. She didn't see the Mad Hatter, but there was plenty of time to find him.

She removed the key ring from his belt and slipped away before he noticed. She was back at the outside of the box a moment later, slipping the key into a large lock on the front. A plan, vague though it was, started to form in her mind. Get Lance and Adam free. Get the Mad Hatter's heart. Return it. Make everyone leave if they hadn't already. She didn't know that she could do much to stop the Queen from getting to Tiger Lily's people, but she might be able to get a warning to them and hopefully they could manage it themselves.

"Halt!" someone cried, Alice throwing herself to the side before the blade could catch her. It clanged against the box and she winced against the sharp shooting pain spreading through her leg.

Alice scrambled back to the lock and turned the key, feeling the click. She quickly grabbed the keys back, turning her attention to the rather casual Mad Hatter. There was no malice in his face, but there was also a sword in his hand getting ready to take another swing at her.

Well. She knew where he was, at least.

Alice reappeared in the black box with Lance and Adam, her mind spinning and trying to remember the plan she had just come up with. Lance was staring with wide eyes at the lid of the box and she wondered if he had heard the sword. "I need to get under the Queen's skirt," she told Adam. "Hearts under the Queen's skirt, right? I'll get the Mad Hatter his heart back and we'll get out of here from there. You guys can open the box now and run for it. I'll meet you back at the White Rabbit's house."

Adam reached into one of his pockets and pulled out a piece of cake and a familiar potion with instruction labels on them.

"You know what, if it gets bad out there, eat this," Adam told Lance, handing him a small cake with a note on it saying *Eat Me*.

"What is this?"

"Trust me," Adam said. "You get in trouble, you eat that."

"I'll take that one," Alice said, grabbing the *Drink Me* vial from Adam. She took a very small sip and thought about the underside of the Queen of Heart's dress as she vanished from inside the box.

CHAPTER 17

The Queen's Behind

ALICE COULDN'T BE that small but, slipping under the queen's skirt, she found it was much larger than she expected it would be. She thought she was as small as the Queen's shin, but the skirt spiralled up high around her. The Queen's legs looked so far away, like far too slender trees that blossomed into bloomers high above her. Instead of hoops of wire holding the shape of the skirt was a spiral of shelves that wound up further and further. A small walkway followed them up, and Alice could swear she saw a small family of mice high above her watching from behind the railings. There were so many things kept on the shelves, knick knacks and much less trivial things, but Alice didn't have time to go through everything she kept under here.

Fortunately, the Queen of Hearts didn't appear to have that kind of time either. The hearts were stored together not too far up on the shelves, each kept in a glass box. Alice hopped onto the walkway and raced up, finding a line of glass boxes each half the size of her and some containing hearts beating inside.

The skirt shifted as she got closer and she clung to the rail of the walkway, keeping herself from tumbling over. Alice started to take another step as the skirt rocked around her, the distant legs dancing in the center of the dome, but stopped herself. There was a much easier way to get there.

Disappearing from her spot, she reappeared in front of the glass boxes and held onto the railing as she looked them over. They all had labels on them, including several that didn't have any hearts in them yet. There was one labeled AMC with a mushroom and sword crossed under it that she had an unsettling feeling meant that Adam was on her list. There was also an AL with a black headband that made Alice reach up and touch her own. So the Queen did remember her.

One engraved with MH and the drawing of a top hat was not far away from those two. She tried to grab it off the shelf, but the box would not budge. She didn't have time for this, the skirt stirring more and more around her. Taking a deep breath, she opened the lid of the box and took the heart, feeling it still warm and pulsing under her fingers. Her stomach turned and she resisted the urge drop it and run. It would only be for a moment.

Alice was back at the box as the skirt jolted again, finding it very different than how she'd left it only a moment before. It had been tipped over, the top of it open to the fighting that had broken out around her. The men whose hearts Alice had returned not long ago were here, and she thought she saw a flash of Tiger Lily among the fray. The White King's men had joined them, several of them amidst the fray looking to annoy the enemy out of the fight. Alice was glad that most of them at least knew how to fight, though their style was entirely flashy and much less direct, offering plenty of chances to block and none to attack. They were also dangerously close to the box, a clang of metal beside her making her jump and hug the heart uncomfortably close to keep from letting it slip out of her small arms.

She needed to get this heart back in the Mad Hatter, but first she needed to be taller to keep from being trampled on. The Queen of Hearts was shrieking across the field and Alice couldn't risk being trampled with the heart. She looked around and spotted Lance easily in the fray, opting for a spot on his shoulder as her next target to keep herself out of trouble.

Lance had grown taller than the trees by a fair margin and was fanatically trying to kick away the people coming for his legs. Alice appeared on his shoulder, grabbing him by the ear to keep herself from falling off. "Hey," she said, trying to balance herself and what felt like a giant heart on his shoulder. "Do you have any of that cake left?"

"You knew what this stuff did?" Lance demanded. He knocked away a few more people, picking them up and using them as a bat against the rest. "This is nuts!"

"Are there nuts in it this time?" Alice asked. "You think it will still work if I pick them out?"

Lance frowned but tried to stay still so Alice could keep her balance, and reached into his pocket to pull out what looked like a very small bit of cake in his hands. It was much larger in Alice's hand and she exchanged it for the potion. "Thanks," she said. "When you want to get small again, just a little of that one."

Taking a bite of the cake, she hopped off of Lance's shoulder and vanished into the fray. She was her usual size when she appeared again, trying to stay out of the way of the fights around her and keep the heart safe. Find the Mad Hatter. Return the heart. Get Lance and Adam out of here. Once that was done, she could leave as well, but first she had to find Hatter.

It didn't take long to track him down. She got to the edge of a ring of people who were avoiding the fight and found Adam with two swords, a knife and a tomahawk holding off the Mad Hatter and the White Knight. At a second glance, Alice realized that he had four arms. And two heads. And two torsos. Somehow, he had managed to split himself down the middle to the hip, and she could only hope he knew how to put himself back together again.

Despite now having two heads, he kept even pace with both of them as they circled around him. He met their swords with his own or blocked with the shorter weapon while trying to strike with the longer one. With the White Knight holding a broadsword and the Mad Hatter holding a far finer blade, it was a feat to see him manage them both.

Alice noticed as they exchanged blows that they moved in a very similar fashion to one another. They were light on their feet and moved deftly, but Adam looked much less afraid to fight dirty, while the Mad Hatter and the White Knight were both more than experienced in very different ways. The White Knight was very straightforward while the Mad Hatter danced about for an opening, Adam looking very might like he could use a third torso, or a second set of legs to keep up for much longer.

He needed help and Alice provided as best she knew how. She reached out and grabbed the sword from the Mad Hatter, snatching it out of his hands and throwing it down on the ground behind her before relieving the White Knight of his. Adam caught sight of her and forced the White Knight into the crowd around them, forcing someone else to engage with him before he knocked the Mad Hatter to the ground. He butt him hard in the face, knocking him out before nodding to Alice.

He'd cover her. She would have the time she needed.

Alice tried to work quickly, blocking out the fight around her and started to work. She knelt next to him with the heart, reminding herself that the Mad Hatter was of Wonderland and the methods to return his heart were different than how she had done it earlier that day. Unlike those of Neverland, a Wonderland heart sought the body instead of the mind seeking the heart to match it.

The words came out easily from her and she was able to send the heart from her hand to his chest easily. The only thing Alice needed to do was keep talking to it and try to coax it back into place on its own. The heart felt rejected after leaving for so long, but Alice was able to convince it that the Mad Hatter wanted it back.

The problem was not that it wouldn't go back, but that it couldn't. There was something in the way as it tried to go through and Alice couldn't break her concentration when she was so close. She kept trying to coax it through, her words getting louder and more insistent, but the heart couldn't break through whatever was keeping it out. Something shoved it sharply aside, and she had to convince it that it had not been rejected and to try again.

And then it was through. Alice lurched forward as it fell

into place and she kept going, coaxing it back into taking its rightful place and talking to the body to make it obey as well. The reunion seemed to be a happy one, bringing the two parts of him together as he relaxed under Alice's fingers and his heart started to beat more comfortably behind the ribcage that it called home.

When it was done, she opened her eyes to find Adam's axe lying on the Mad Hatter's chest next to a very large hole in his armour. Adam was up again, fighting the White Knight and three more playing cards. He split again from the waist, now with three heads and six arms working independently to keep her safe.

Alice caught her breath and looked around, her eyes catching on something in the sky. There was something coming towards them, large and familiar with one riding on its back and another climbing up the tail of it. She smacked Adam on the leg and got the attention of one of his heads. "Jabber-wocky," Alice said, pointing up at the sky.

Alice looked down at the Mad Hatter, still unconscious and probably not the best sight for the Jabberwocky to come back to when it showed up. She couldn't drag him away, not through all this fighting, and Alice couldn't remember the spells to keep the Jabberwocky in check just now. Not that she knew them much anymore, since they were all in a book she no longer had.

"We have to get the Mad Hatter out," Adam said. "Get Lance. He'll manage."

"You too," Alice said, glancing back at the forces. "The Queen of Hearts wants you too."

Adam shook his head, but Alice was already gone, back on Lance's shoulder. He had not shrunk yet, but he was doing much better now. His legs were bleeding, but he didn't appear to be in much danger, now just kicking them off and looking more annoyed than anything.

"Need to get Adam and the Hatter out of here," she told him. "Grab a fridge. They should both fit."

"Sure," Lance said, clearly having given up on getting any of this to make sense. He reached over into the trees and pulled a large one, ripping the door off of it, and walked over to where Adam still fought too many foes. Lance knocked the White Knight away with the door and kept using it to keep the rest off of their backs while Adam and Alice worked to get the Mad Hatter into the fridge.

Adam popped something into his mouth and his torsos fell back into one, each of his arms pocketing or hiding their various weapons as he came back together. Adam pushed the Mad Hatter into the back of the fridge before hopping in behind him. Lance picked them up and Adam grabbed Alice, pulling her in with a yelp as Lance picked them up. Lance knocked the trees away and tried to rush them away from the fighting.

"Far enough!" Adam called up to him. "Alice, do you still have—"

"Already gave the potion back to him," Alice said as Lance put them back down on the ground. Lance shrank down next to them a moment later, looking shaken. He looked haggard and far worse for wear, though Adam looked like he'd taken more than his fair share of cuts and jabs, freely bleeding from his arms despite how carelessly he was holding himself.

"How you doing?" Adam asked him, putting a gloved hand on his brother's shoulder and giving it a light rub.

"I hate this place," Lance told him.

"Don't try to murder anyone again and you won't have to come back."

Lance shot a venomous glare at Adam, but there was no time for a response. Behind them, Alice heard a cry of "*Off with her head!*" coming from a very furious Queen of Hearts, followed by a stampede of footsteps coming in their direction. Through the trees, Alice could see the Queen's troop was coming for them.

"Get the Mad Hatter out of here," Alice said, her mind already working. "The Jabberwocky liked him. I don't think he's going to be happy if he finds out we busted open his nose. Just get to the White Rabbit's house."

"And where do you think you're going?" Adam said, grabbing her by the arm before she had a chance to leave. "You're still not looking so hot."

She knew he was right. She still felt light headed and she was limping, but she couldn't stop now. "Jabberwocky," Alice said.

"It doesn't like you."

"Too bad for it." Alice pulled her arm away and disappeared back to the battle. She needed to get the Queen away from them first, and lead them to the Jabberwocky. By that time, she hoped that she could think of something.

Alice appeared at the Queen's side, standing next to her on the platform as it moved very slowly behind the troop of men. She was standing in the box now being pulled by several cards, her face flushed a deep, angry red. They were being stopped at the sides by the White King's people, who seemed entirely too giddy to be involved in fisticuffs.

"Whose head are you demanding?" Alice asked innocently, looking at the people around her.

"That wretched child's," the Queen told her, anger dripping off of every word. "Abysmal manners, and *thievery* of all things. She must be punished."

"She sounds pretty awful." Alice wasn't comfortable with how fast they were moving, even with the opposition. "If we're being clear, this child is myself, am I correct? I am a pretty awful child. My parents say so."

The Queen looked down and Alice was not aware that nostrils could flare just that widely. She tried to grab her, though Alice vanished and appeared outside of her reach. "Return!" the Queen bellowed as she tried to grab her again, Alice disappearing off of the box entirely and appearing where she could watch her next to a tree. "You have all let her escape! *I demand her head!*"

Alice made her escape very deliberately, lingering in each spot just long enough for someone to state that they had spotted her before vanishing again. She had no desire to burn Wonderland down or cause it any more harm than she already had, heading to the open space of the plains to flag down the Jabberwocky.

The Jabberwocky had no such reservations, to say the least as it flew overhead. It cast flame down on both sides, sending them both scattering with their heads on fire in most cases. It swooped down low and Alice could see someone riding its back, trying to calm it down, though it looked like it was still in a frenzy as it thrashed about in the air. Calming a little, but there was still work to be done.

She saw one person drop off the Jabberwocky who wasn't the rider and knew who this one was. Her long black hair and the knife in each hand made her entirely distinctive. Tiger Lily joined the fray, making quick work of anyone who dared come too close.

Alice got to Tiger Lily as soon as there was a lull, appearing in front of her and putting her hands up. Alice kept having to move around her as she talked, narrowly avoiding getting hurt as the Queen's men engaged her in battle and pulled her this way and that. "Mad Hatter has his heart back," Alice said. "Who's on the Jabberwocky?"

Tiger Lily smiled a strange smile that Alice wondered was driven largely by the fact that she was enjoying the fight in front of her. "You keep interesting company, Alice of Wonderland," she said. "Even if they do smell." She was gone a moment later, jumping at another man and starting to bark orders at the recovered Natives.

Once it finally touched down on the ground, Alice appeared behind the dragon and looked up to find Adrianna riding on the back of the Jabberwocky. She leaned forward and spoke softly to him, stroking him gently to get him to calm down. The Jabberwocky swung around, catching Alice with his tail and throwing her back into a tree. Her head smacked hard into the trunk and stars dotted her vision as the Jabberwocky turned on her, growling menacingly.

"Alice!" Adrianna said from atop the dragon. "No! You leave her alone! She's not going to hurt you."

The Jabberwocky backed off at that. Adrianna stroked him gently on the neck as chaos continued around her and smiled down at Alice before concern dominated her face. Despite the knock to her head, Alice was very aware of the pain in her neck and the blood running down her leg.

"What happened?" Adrianna asked.

"We have to get out of here," Alice said, not daring to move any closer to a Jabberwocky that still clearly didn't like her very much. "Lance and Adam are on the way to the White Rabbit's. You should go meet up with…"

Alice trailed off. The Queen's men may be dispersing, but many of them were heading through the woods. Adrianna wouldn't be safe running through it on her own, even if she did know where she was going. She needed someone to take her through the woods. "Wait here."

Alice went back through the battle until she found Tiger Lily, chasing a few more people away and looking almost disappointed. Alice put her hands up as Tiger Lily turned on her, and Tiger Lily put down her knives. "Can you get Adrianna out of here?" Alice asked. "She can't be here."

"Adrianna controls the Jabberwocky," Tiger Lily said. "She is best suited here until the Queen of Hearts is no longer a problem."

"Fine," Alice said tightly, going back around to see Adrianna again. Another plan. She could do this.

Alice appeared in front of the Jabberwocky with her hands up. The Jabberwocky snapped at her, but Adrianna pulled him back before he could do anything more "Adrianna?" she called up to her. "Can you ask the Jabberwocky to pick up that thing over there and drop it off at the Queen of Heart's castle?"

Adrianna followed Alice's finger to the box now crawling out of the woods toward them. "Sure," she said, getting off the neck of the Jabberwocky. She spoke to it gently, stroking it all the while and making gestures to tell it what to pick up and where to drop it off. The Jabberwocky seemed to listen to her well and it took off, plucking the box off of the platform. The lid slammed shut as it turned under his claws and the Jabberwocky flew off with it.

"Make this thing put me down!" the Queen of Hearts bellowed of her soldiers as she was carried away. All of those in earshot were quick to drop what they were doing and obey her, chasing after the flying box and the dragon that carried it back to the castle.

Alice grabbed Adrianna by the arm and pulled her through the remaining people after them. "We have to get you out of here," Alice said, bringing her out of the way to safety. "Tiger Lily!"

"What's going on?" Adrianna asked her. "I think I tried to hurt you before. Your neck..."

"Not the time," Alice said quickly. "There's kind of been a huge battle here and they're not all gone yet. You need to leave before you get hurt."

"What about you?" she asked. "You can protect me if something bad happens, right? But nothing bad is going to happen."

Tiger Lily appeared and shook her head at Alice and Adrianna, though a smile played on her lips. "You keep very interesting company, Alice of Wonderland," she said, leading them both through the forest. "Where has Adam and his brother taken the Mad Hatter?"

"They should be going to the White Rabbit's house," Alice said. "Do you know where I can find a mirror?"

"I am sure you will be able to find that as well, Alice of Wonderland."

"I'm going to make sure they made it," Alice told her, stepping away in search of two boys and a refrigerator.

CHAPTER 18

A Moment to Breathe

THE WHITE RABBIT was not at his house, though everyone else was when Alice finally arrived. After a while, she had forgotten where she was going until she stumbled across the house. She took a seat outside, away from the people with no hearts, and caught her breath. She was only just realizing how exhausting it was to constantly get knocked out and run around when she was still recovering from being choked to death with a shoelace. And having a bear trap around her leg. And being smacked hard in the head.

"I am amazed you don't have a concussion yet," Adam muttered as Tiger Lily tended to the injuries that Alice didn't think needed any attention. She protested for only a moment before Adrianna asked her to let them, looking so guilty that Alice stopped all together. Adam was busy next to her, putting leaves on Lance's few cuts and wrapping them up. He was still limping himself from where he took something in the leg, but no one seemed to be concerned about patching him up right now. They had left the Mad Hatter inside, sure that he would let them know as soon as he woke up. "Or that you've been as lucky as you've been."

"It doesn't hurt anymore," Alice said, wincing as Tiger Lily put a salve on her neck. "You don't have to do that."

"Yes she does," Adam told her. "Someone is going to notice you all beat up with a bear trap mark on your leg, scratches all over your arms and a rope burn on your neck."

"You are much more injured than you realize, Alice of Wonderland," Tiger Lily said, holding her shoulder whenever Alice twitched just a little too much.

"I need to find a mirror," Alice said. "Someone is going to notice that Lance and Adrianna have disappeared. I don't even know how long we've been gone for, but Joe and Travis probably noticed that we aren't in their room anymore. We never did make it to dinner."

"It might not be a good idea for them to go back yet, Alice," Adam said.

"Why not?" Adrianna asked, her voice quiet. She was still trying to process everything that had happened since she got there. She was horrified that so many people had gotten hurt and didn't know what she was supposed to do about any of it, not knowing how to do much in terms of the first aid and

Tiger Lily not trusting her to help because of the way she smelled.

"Right, you missed that part," Adam said, tying up the last of the bandages on Lance and setting back down to finally fix his own leg. "Because Claudia might have made both of you turn on Alice. Apparently Alice took one of her books and it looks like she is trying to get it back. A green one?"

Adam reached over and smacked Lance, who was already starting to go into a bit of a trance from the idea that Alice took something from Claudia. Adrianna didn't have the same reaction, her eyes going down and squinting at the ground like it might remind her. She shook her head, unable to come up with anything. "I don't..."

"It's okay," Adam said, motioning her closer and offering him a one armed hug while he pulled a length of cloth over a patch of leaves. "It sounds like things are pretty crazy on that side as they are over here sometimes. Just be careful over there. Maybe we'll just keep Lance over here," he added to Lance.

"I didn't know what I was doing!" Lance exclaimed, throwing his one good arm up in the air. "Do I look like you? I'm not going to try to murder someone!"

"You saying I'd murder someone?" Adam asked, perfectly calm, but his voice becoming very dark.

Alice pulled herself up and out of Tiger Lily's gentle hands and was gone before she could grab her back. She needed a mirror and she was going to find one, but she also needed to clear her head. It hurt to put much weight on her leg, but she continued to do it anyway. She needed to move.

Her mind wandered too much at first to bring her near a mirror. She walked along the shore of the lake, through a freezer full of ice, and past some particularly shiny rocks, none of them quite what she was looking for. Her leg hurt with every step and her head pounded, but she needed to be away for just a few moments. Her fingers trailed to her neck, and Adam's words echoed in her mind. She wondered how much it really mattered.

"And what will you do when they come back for you?" the Cheshire Cat asked, appearing next to her time and again as she continued to wander. "And make no mistake, your friends will turn on you again."

"I'll deal with it when it happens," Alice said, continuing to walk. The Cheshire Cat reminded her that there were people waiting for her. A mirror. She needed one she could bring back. The glassy surface of the lake would not cut it. The shiny rocks were not large enough.

"Still so sure that they will help," Cat said.

"I only need to survive until the end of the school year," Alice told him. "After that, it won't matter anymore."

"Is that when you give up?" Cat asked. She could almost hear the sneer in his voice as he spoke.

"Yes."

Cat didn't follow her after that. Alice kept looking around until finally she came across a dressing room that had been abandoned long enough for a thick layer of dust to build up over everything. She pushed the clothing off of it and onto the floor, not caring whose it might have been or if they would ever return for it. If they asked and she was still around, she would bring it back. For now, she grabbed hold of it and headed back to the White Rabbit's house.

"Okay," Alice said, putting the mirror down between them all. "Time to go back home."

"Where did you get that?" Lance asked.

"Found it. Come on."

Alice started flipping through the mirror to find one this one would connect to back to somewhere safe on campus. It reflected part of the pond back up at them first and Alice tried to think of what else she could check. Should she bother with her own room again, or would there still be people in there trying to repair it? Lance didn't live in that room any longer, but was it abandoned enough that she could still use it anyway? It looked dark out, but was it actually dark enough for people to be sleeping yet?

"Aren't you worried we're just going to start breaking into your room and trying to kill you again as soon as we get back?" Lance demanded.

"I'll be fine," Alice told him. "Adrianna will beat you up if you try it again.'

"This is serious, Alice."

"Oh, they got the mirrors back in our room," Alice said, flipping to her own room. There were shapes moving in the darkness, looking through things. Alice wondered if they were just working, though it was strange that they would be working in such darkness. "You think the power's out again?" Alice asked. "They don't usually work in the dark, do they?"

"That looks an awful lot like Travis," Adam said, looking over her shoulder.

"It is!" Adrianna confirmed. "And Joe's over there too. Why are they in our room?"

"Probably looking for the book again," Lance said. "Joe's probably going to break stuff if we don't stop them."

"Go on," Alice said. "You guys go ahead first."

'We'll give you the all clear when you can come back. Adam, you coming?"

"I have stuff to do here still," he said. "I'm sure you can handle them."

Lance nodded, though he didn't look happy about it. He led Adrianna through the mirror as another figure appeared in the window that had been left open in the cool November night. Alice didn't bother being worried anymore, waving at the figure from the mirror and making sure he saw the two of them walking through so he wouldn't be overwhelmed.

Alice turned around and her eyes rested for only a moment on Tiger Lily before settling on Adam. "Four months," she told him. "Finish whatever you have to do, and then you come back over."

"Addie seems to think you're working on this whole Bandersnatch thing," Adam told her coldly. "If you are, then it shouldn't matter when I come back. You'll always be able to come back for me."

"Adrianna has too much faith in me," Alice told him, not quite able to meet his eyes. "Four months. Try to find Matt, too. I'll be back for the rest of the people in the White Rabbit's house." She stepped back through the mirror before she could be stopped by either of them.

CHAPTER 19

Last Winter

WHEN ALICE WALKED back through, Joe and Travis were both ready to pounce on Lance when Peter flew up behind them. He clapped his hands over both of their mouths and shoved something into them before he pulled them backwards so hard they hit the ground. They bounced off the ground, but they didn't move after that.

"Hello Peter," Alice said brightly, though she knew she looked like awful. "How have you been?"

Peter looked at her long and hard. "I told you I didn't like them," he said. "They smell like her."

Adrianna looked worried. "Do I smell bad?" she asked. "Tiger Lily said I smelled funny too. I mean, I haven't showered in a while. Maybe I just need to take a shower?"

"How long have we been gone?" Alice asked. "Please don't say weeks."

Peter shrugged. "It's Thursday when the sun comes up," he said.

"Not too bad," Alice muttered. That left a good four days before school started again and that would give her enough time to figure out some way of covering up her scars a little better than not at all. "Only a few days this time."

"What did you do to them?" Lance asked, looking down at his unconscious brothers.

"Oh," Peter said. "There's this plant thing that Tiger Lily showed me once. You're supposed to use it to make people not crazy anymore, so I found some of it and gave it to them. You're welcome."

Alice didn't know if that was a *Thank you* sort of moment, but she would not protest. If this meant that she wouldn't have to deal with the pair of them attacking her looking for the book, then she was happy. Instead, Lance took the lead on the questioning while she knelt down to poke at them to see if they were going to wake up.

"Where did you get the plant?" Lance asked.

"It's growing by the pond," Peter said, looking him over carefully and not bothering to keep his feet on the ground as he looked him over. "What happened to you? You look like you fought pirates and lost. Did you go fighting pirates without me?"

"Have you always been able to fly?" Adrianna asked.

"Alice didn't tell you?" he asked. "Or was I not supposed to tell them? They just came out of the mirror."

"Peter is from Neverland," Alice said. "Can you bring them back to their own room?"

"Can't you? You're... Did someone try to kill you?" Peter asked, his eyes falling on her neck and looking carefully at it. "You are really bad at fighting pirates. You should probably come and let Tasha show you how to keep them from killing you."

"So you *can* get them out of here," Alice said.

Peter made a sour face and looked to Lance. "Girls are always so bossy," he said, picking up Travis and flying him out the window.

"Don't get caught flying!" Alice called back to him and she turned back to sit on her bed. She laid back and reached a hand around the side of her bed, stroking the books in their hiding spot in the ceiling and patting the Mad Hatter's hat before bringing her hand back. Still there. She would have to return the hat next time she was back over there.

"Books are still safe," she said, sitting back up. "You think we can just stay here until morning?"

"It is our room," Adrianna said.

"But they didn't give us the key yet. We probably shouldn't even be in here. You think we're supposed to still be sleeping in Sarah and Heather's room? What do they think happened to us?"

"We might have gone on vacation," Lance suggested. "And there was an accident and that's what happened to you and me."

"Somehow I don't think an accident is enough to explain everything," Alice said, her fingers going up to her neck. It hurt, she realized now that the adrenaline rush was coming down, when she touched it and when she moved her neck too much too quickly. She could still feel the phantom of the shoelace on her neck and she was still surprised that she wasn't bleeding more from the attack. "It's a good start, though," she conceded. She didn't have anything better, and hadn't even thought of how to explain Lance's condition.

"Alice?" Adrianna asked. She kept looking at Joe's body unconscious on the floor with the yellow flower sticking out of his mouth. "If I do anything like that again, you know you can stop me, right? You know you can hit me."

"Me too," Lance said.

Alice nodded. "I'll be sure to do that next time," she said, not bothering to remind them that they had both taken her completely by surprise and restrained her before she could have done anything. She rubbed at her arms where Adrianna's nails dug in and couldn't quite stop herself from thinking the worst. Between holding a heart and everything else that had happened, she now found herself worried that one or both of them would turn on her as soon as she closed her eyes.

"Alice can't punch someone," Peter's voice came from the window as he flew back in. "Look at her. She doesn't know how to do anything. She just gets mad and leaves."

Alice glared at Peter but said nothing, knowing he was right. He looked back and forth between Alice and Lance and Adrianna, slowly piecing together what happened, though Alice was very careful to move her neck so that he couldn't stare at the rope burn.

Peter went to Lance and flew up so that he was hovering just a little above him, looking down at him accusingly. "Were *you* the one that tried to kill her?" he asked. He laughed at that more than he was mad, though Lance still looked ashamed about it. "You let him?"

"I didn't *let* him," Alice protested. "I just couldn't exactly leave." She was very careful not to look at Adrianna, though she couldn't help but keep rubbing her arms as she talked. "It's none of your business, Peter. Just get Joe back to his room."

"I can teach you to fight him," Peter said, crossing his legs and floating upside down in the air as he pointed back at Lance, who looked like he didn't believe Peter at all. "He's way scrawnier than the pirates back in Neverland. You won't even need a sword for him! Or you can ask Tasha."

"I can't get a permission slip," Alice said carefully, meeting Peter's eyes and he rolled his own in response.

"Fine," he said. "*I'll* teach you. I'm better than everyone in there anyway. If you're going to save Neverland for me, then you should at least know how to punch someone in the face when they try to do whatever he tried to do to you."

"Just get Joe back to his room," Alice told Peter. Peter took the hint this time, winking at her and picking up Joe on the way out of there. Alice was getting tired, but there was one more place she needed to go. She got to her feet and stayed there, addressing Adrianna and Lance first.

"I'm going to see Sarah," Alice said. "I think we're supposed to be in there for now. I'll get them to let you in, but I need to talk to Sarah first, okay?"

Adrianna nodded, Lance looking at her strangely. "Sarah?"

"She was taken by the Bandersnatch like Evan," Adrianna said. "She owes Alice for that."

Alice nodded. "You should head back to your own room and get some sleep. You can get across campus without getting caught, right?"

Lance hesitated before he nodded. Alice thought it was pity that was on his face, or maybe he just saw how close she was to dropping that he let it go and headed out. Adrianna followed him out, taking a seat at the front of Heather and Sarah's door. She hoped Lance would be able to sleep off most of his injuries so that he didn't have to deal with too many questions.

Alice took a step toward the wall and was at Sarah's bedside. Alice and Adrianna's cots were still on the floor. Both Sarah and Heather were fast asleep, Sarah snoring while Heather had ear plugs in to keep from hearing Sarah at all during the night. Alice put her hand over Sarah's mouth before she shook her awake.

Sarah jolted up, letting out a yelp under her hand, but calmed down as soon as she saw Alice. Alice nodded for the washroom, looking back at Heather before Sarah nodded.

"Where have you been?" Sarah demanded in a whisper as soon as the washroom door closed. "Adrianna's brothers said you were picked up by Adrianna's step mother for a trip, but you never came back from— Oh my god."

Alice turned on the light and Sarah fell silent as she looked at what had become of Alice. Alice was sure she was looking worse as the adrenaline keeping her upright drained from her. Sarah reached out a moment towards Alice's neck before pulling her hand backwards sharply. "Does it have to do with…"

Alice nodded, letting her come to her own conclusions. It did technically have to do with the Bandersnatch if she went back on it far enough. "Can you make my neck look like nothing happened?" Alice asked. "I can do the rest, but I don't have anything for that."

Sarah hesitated for a long moment before she started to speak again. "You have to promise me," she said. "Promise me, Alice. This is the last time any of this ever happens. I do this and you never do anything that's going to get you this hurt or injured ever again."

"It's not like I wanted to—"

"*Promise me.*"

Alice swallowed her words and nodded. "I promise," she said.

Sarah let her shoulders drop and the breath escape her. "I'll do what I can in the morning," she said, her gentle hands turning Alice's neck and face to get a better look. "And mom's working on a new line of stuff that has, like, Polysporin and stuff in them so they can help with cuts and stuff. I'll call her to get her to send me a bunch in your colour and it'll be here in a day. I don't know if I have enough for all this right now, though. Seriously, Alice, what happened to you?"

Alice wavered on her feet. She didn't have much time before she would pass out and she was clinging to consciousness as it was. "I can just wear long sleeves and tights for the rest of it," she said. "And Adrianna's right outside the door. Can we stay here tonight?"

"Of course Adrianna's involved," Sarah said. "She better not be as bad as you are."

Alice only heard the first two words before she let herself drop, falling and landing on the cot that was for herself. Despite the thoughts running through her head, sleep came quickly and she was quick to accept its sweet embrace.

THE NEXT MORNING, Alice and Adrianna were let back into their room. Both Adrianna and Sarah insisted on letting Alice sleep, buried deep under the covers until everyone had left for the day. Sarah slipped up a little later to wake her up and apply her makeup to make sure no one noticed that she was sporting a huge mark, as well as teaching Alice a couple of tricks.

The makeup she ordered from her mother, on the other hand, was a bust. Alice wasn't sure if it was the makeup itself or the course brushes she was given to help her apply it, but she broke out into a rash that covered and explained away the mark on her neck. She was covered in blotches on her face for the next week while school faded back into normal. Sarah felt guilty for it, but Alice insisted that it was all for the best.

The break seemed to calm everything down and Alice no longer had to worry about anyone breaking into her room. Lance found the flower and took it upon himself to regularly eat some of it just in case, as well as slip it to Travis and Joe to keep them from falling back into those habits. Adrianna didn't show any sign that she was hypnotized yet, but Alice kept a few flowers with her just in case.

Alice sank into studying with everyone else, finals more than clearing her mind of everything else. She didn't want to deal with Wonderland right now, and she didn't bother going back at all on Adam's insistence. And Lance's. Lance seemed much more protective and worried since seeing just how much damage she could have done to herself when she was over there, not to mention how injured he had been. Eventually he had to go to the doctor to get himself patched up properly, the leaves only helping for the day before it was time to change them again.

The semester passed quietly. With the winter weather settling in, everyone was pretty content to let Alice stay inside and study instead of going out to play in the snow. They had their own grades and classes to worry about leading up to the winter formal.

They headed out in a group, but Alice retreated quickly to the side of the room. She watched everyone else having fun, Adrianna and everyone else having the time of their lives and enjoying their last year of middle school before they moved on to the next chapter. They chattered on excitedly about how it was only one more term and they would be in high school, about how much would change and how nothing would change at all.

Alice excused herself to the washroom shortly into the night and appeared on the roof surrounded by the small garden. The snow had covered it, but this time she had boots and a jacket so she could stay for a while in the quiet where she would not be bothered. Alice felt better already about the silence and she was happy to let it engulf her. Still, she needed something else here.

She should be enjoying the company of her friends. She might not get much longer to see them, what with the Bandersnatch in the woods just waiting to take her away, but she couldn't handle all the people. They were all so concerned about her. For how little they said, she felt like they were watching her and paying much more attention to what she was doing. Maybe in the new year they would be better.

Her parents didn't want her to come back home for Christmas this year. Adrianna's family would take her instead, which meant that she would get more time with Lori. She would have liked to spend some time with her parents before she vanished, but they were busy with the divorce. She had to accept that she probably would never get a proper chance to say goodbye to them. No matter. She would deal with it all later.

It also meant being in the same house as Claudia. Alice hoped that Claudia wouldn't mind her back and wouldn't set the entire family on her while she was there. She wasn't sure if she could do anything against Lori if she tried to put a shoelace around her neck and tried to kill her. She might just let her finish the job that Lance failed to do.

She was getting ahead of herself, though. Claudia might leave her alone entirely while she was there. She might not even be there in the first place, like she wasn't there during summer. She might have nothing to worry about and Alice could just have a nice, quiet time for the break to enjoy everyone's company.

It wouldn't happen, of course. But she could hope. Maybe she could work really hard on learning the curse book over the next couple days to figure out a way to protect herself until the new year. There did appear to be a lot of interesting stuff in there that Claudia may not have seen. She didn't know what half the stuff in the book was yet and she was anxious to actually dive into it.

Alice looked up, finding Peter flying in on her private spot. He took a perch on the roof instead of coming in and disturbing the gently falling snow around her. He was quick to plop his butt into what was on the roof and looked down at her, chin resting in his hands and waiting for her to do something.

"Hi," she said, looking up at him curiously. "Not going to the dance?"

"It's boring!" he said. "And girls are such a pain. One asked me to go with her, but she wants me to keep dancing with her to all the slow stuff and it's boring. So I thought, you know what I said I would do? I'd teach Alice how to not suck in a fight. And here I am."

"How did you find me?"

"I am a master of hide and seek," Peter told her. "And you know what else I have?"

He paused for dramatic effect before he brought a key out of his pocket.

"Tasha's key to the gym."

"Can we really be in there?" Alice asked, though a smile danced across her face.

"If we don't get caught. I'll race you!"

Alice watched Peter zoom off and smiled as she took a single step over, appearing in the gym. She turned the light on for them to work with, none of the lights in this room extending outside except through the skylight. She doubted anyone would notice tonight with the dance going on. She waited until she heard the rattling of keys at the door and Peter let himself in.

"Hey, no fair!" he said, letting himself in, though he wasn't the least bit bothered by it. Alice put down her heavy winter clothing on the bleachers and took off her shoes, staying in her dance attire otherwise with makeup and hair done up while Peter did the same.

They spent the next hour going over the basics of how to throw a punch and how to block, Peter not having the patience to hold back when he took swings at her himself. Alice picked it up fast enough, finding most of it a lot easier than she thought and she was not afraid of hitting Peter back after the number of times she had been smacked so far.

Eventually, it devolved into just circling one another, ready to hit one another. She was having trouble with it, finding it more difficult to remember everything she learned while Peter moved so easily. She spent so much time blocking that she forgot to attack and kept waiting for his next blow to come. Finally, Peter let out a very loud sigh.

"Would you disappear already?" he asked. "No one out there is going to be holding back what they can do."

"Isn't that cheating?" Alice asked.

Peter lifted off the ground and pulled a sword off the wall before returning to her. "Of course it is," he said. "But there's no such thing as cheating in a fight."

Alice smiled widely and side stepped her way to the other side of the room when he lunged forward. Finally, she was having some fun tonight. Finally.

About the Author

TANYA LISLE IS a novelist from Metro Vancouver, British Columbia, who has series littered across genres from supernatural horror to young adult fantasy. She began writing in elementary school, when she started turning homework assignments into short stories and continued this trend well into university. While attending Simon Fraser University, she developed an appreciation for public domain crossovers and cross-platform narratives. She has a shelf full of notebooks with more story ideas than pens lost to the depths of her bag. Now she writes incessantly in hopes of finishing all of them.

Thankfully, her cat, Remy, has figured out how to shut off Tanya's computer when she needs to take a break.

www.ingramcontent.com/pod-product-compliance
Lightning Source LLC
Chambersburg PA
CBHW031053020726
47495CB00007B/1849